The Art of Secrets

From the award-winning author, recipient of:

Indie B.R.A.G medallion
Chill with a Book Readers' Award
Gold Standard Quality Mark

"The art of great writing! ... Adin keeps a tight rein on her leading characters, their actions and reactions credibly grounded in genuine emotions. The change of tone from Emma to Charlotte, from young to old, works, helps the reader see behind the lies and half-truths they tell each other. Their progress from antagonists to friends is seamless, as the layers of the story peel back like petals, exposing the truth at the flower's heart."

– Bev Robitai, author of *Sunstrike*

The Art of Secrets

Vicky Adin

THE ART OF SECRETS

ISBN 978-0-9941035-7-4

To order copies of this book please visit www.vickyadin.co.nz
Also available from www.amazon.com, www.createspace.com
Ebook available from www.amazon.com

First produced for Vicky Adin in 2014 by
AM Publishing New Zealand www.ampublishingnz.com

Other books by Vicky Adin (see p. 241)

The Cornish Knot
Brigid The Girl from County Clare
Gwenna The Welsh Confectioner
The Disenchanted Soldier

Children's book by Vicky Adin

Kazam!

Dedication

To those who suffered
and those who learnt to survive

Acknowledgements

The last words written appear at the front of a book because they are the most important. Without the assistance of many people, this book could not have happened. I am certain that in naming individuals I will miss some I should have included, so please take it as given – if you have assisted me in any way, I am deeply grateful.

I thank the members of the Mairangi Writers' Group who listened, critiqued and helped improve the storyline and language, but especially Jenny Harrison and Erin McKechnie, great authors in their own right, and also fellow author Stephanie Hammond, who as my beta-readers gave me valuable feedback.

I am indebted to Adrienne Morris, publisher, proofreader and editor extraordinaire, for her skill in ensuring this book is as flawless as humanly possible. Any remaining errors are mine and mine alone.

As a genealogist I give tribute to families and their life stories everywhere. Research uncovers many family histories that deserve to be put into print and *The Art of Secrets* is an amalgam of those stories – stories of tragedy and loss, of conflict and resolution, and of personal renewal.

Lastly, to my own wonderful family – my husband, children and grandchildren – thank you. Your belief in me keeps me going.

Part One

The present and the past

"But he who dares not grasp the thorns
should never crave the rose."
– Anne Brontë

Emma

November

"I can't do this any more, Jackie."

Jacqueline McKenzie looked up sharply from her computer and peered at me across the top of her glasses. "I'll pretend I didn't hear that, Emma, but it's crunch time. I can't hold the position open any longer. I need to hear you say you're coming back."

As editor of a large New Zealand woman's magazine, she could make the hard-nosed decisions with the best of them, but in spite of that, I liked her. She had been my mentor for the dozen or so years since I'd started as a junior. As she'd climbed the ladder, I'd followed in her wake until my life had fallen apart.

I bit my bottom lip, struggling to stay in control. "I can't write a single word that has any meaning. And editing is driving me to drink. I can't concentrate."

Jacqueline took her glasses off and held them partially folded in her hand – a message she was busy. "Steady on. It can't be that bad."

"How the hell do you do it, Jackie?" I asked, angrily wiping away the tears. "You always look so damn cool and collected, while I can't hold myself together for five minutes."

I usually loved gazing at the view overlooking Wellington Harbour from her office, but now I hardly gave it a second glance. I flapped my arms and paced the room before flopping into a chair, hands over my face.

Jacqueline put down her glasses and leaned back into her large executive chair.

"Look, I know you've had a hard time. And I've done my best to understand and support you. But ... It's been how long now? Two, three years?"

I nodded, whispering, "I can't come back."

"Now you listen to me, young lady," she said, leaning forward over the desk. "If you keep on like this you will wreck your career. It's time you pulled yourself together. You used up all your holiday and sick leave; I gave you additional leave and let you go on half time. Those contract and editing jobs were supposed to give you the freedom to sort yourself out. You've come and gone to suit yourself, and I've supported you. Yet here you are again still in a mess. What more do you want? Quite frankly, I'm losing patience with you, my girl."

Put that way I could almost understand her frustration. "You've been more than generous, and I know I'm letting you down, but I just can't seem to do anything right. I don't know what's the matter with me."

"I'll tell you what I think. I think you need a change of scenery and something else to think about other than what's gone wrong in your life. You need to get over it, Emma. I've got an idea. Something I've been thinking about for a while. How about you write some articles for me?"

"What articles?"

She hesitated. "I'm considering something along the lines of 'What ever happened to ...?' or 'Where are they now ...?' on people from the past. Something a bit different. There'd be quite a lot of research involved."

"Really? You want to write about ancient history in your magazine?" This idea was way outside the norm and so unlike her. "Come on, Jackie. This is a modern magazine. Why would you want anything historical?"

She ignored me.

"Here's your first assignment," she said. Switching to her no-frills, no-nonsense manner of getting a job done, she gave me some background material, including an autographed photo of a toddler in a frilly white dress, wearing a bangle, taken around the 1920s by the look of it.

I stared at the photo. Its old-fashioned imagery should have been softly blurred and in sepia tones, but as a modern black-and-white reprint, it was sharp-edged and didn't look right. I felt certain I had seen this image somewhere before but couldn't place it, and the name scrawled across it meant nothing.

"Charlotte Day?" I queried, looking at the signature. "Who's she?"

"A famous author. Don't you read?"

I shrugged. "You want me to track her down and interview her?"

"I do."

"How the hell am I going to do that from a baby photo?"

She handed me a business card.

"Who's this?"

"Ray Morris manages Charlotte Day now. Talk to him and see what he can do to help. I knew him in journalism school back in the dark ages. His nickname was 'Prince Smarmy' and I bet he hasn't changed, so watch out."

Belatedly, I realised I'd been cleverly upstaged. But something about that photo bothered me. For starters, why would anyone use a photo of a child as a promotional photo? It didn't make sense. But it was more than that – the photo seemed familiar somehow, and I needed to know why. My curiosity was aroused.

"Find out what's happened to her. Dig up some dirt. Anything you think will make a good story. Here's a list of a few other has-beens you could follow up and write something on. Ray might be able to help there, too. Some will be short articles; others, like Charlotte Day I hope, could turn into a series. I'll pay you a retainer and put you on contract for six months."

I still hadn't spoken.

"Well, go on. Get on with it."

Galvanised by the new assignment and with no one left to keep me in Wellington, I packed up what few possessions I had and headed north. I knew I wouldn't be back. Thanks to Jackie's generosity, I had enough money to live on for the next six months at least. After that, I would live on my savings if I had to. That was the only benefit to come out of the mess. Nothing else: no home, no roots, no anchors – just money.

I contacted Ray Morris within a few days of arriving in Auckland. "Sorry, sweetie. You'll have to wait until January."

Dismayed I had to wait so long, I pushed for a date and promised to contact him again.

Christmas in Auckland was awful. I spent my time in bars and nightclubs pretending I was young and hip with a fantastic future ahead of me. I went home alone. I did the tourist thing, trying to get to know the city, but returned to my flat bored and frustrated. I resorted to doing some research on Charlotte Day and her fellow has-beens and began to be a little intrigued, but mostly I wasted time, unsettled and confused.

I met Ray on a hot summer's day on Auckland's waterfront. The place was bustling with people, boats were coming and going in the harbour and the gentle sea breeze cooled my shoulders. He arrived late, but as soon as he approached the open-air bar where we'd agreed to meet, I knew it was him; a man in his late forties, tall, trim, suave, and so damn sure of himself. He took his sunglasses off and tugged at his shirt collar, pausing to see if anyone was looking at him before heading my way.

I stood extending my hand. "Mr Morris? I'm Emma Wade."

"Sweetie. Call me Ray." Ignoring my hand, he grasped my shoulders and kissed me first on one cheek then the other. His hands lingered a little too long on my bare arms. "So, you're the little entrepreneur. Nice." His eyes scanned my body.

I smiled as sweetly as I could.

The waiter delivered our drinks and I launched into my plan. "I'd like to follow you around for a few months," I lied, putting my hand on his forearm. "Gathering material for a story about what a publicist and manager does and how you promote your clients. I understand you are the best in the industry."

"Of course I am, sweetie. Now what can I do to help?"

I pretended to think. "Who is your most famous client? That would be a good angle." I leant forward; his eyes followed my fingers as I played with the pendant dangling above my cleavage. "I might even be able to swing an exclusive, and maybe a reward." Knowing I wouldn't. I could play the game as well as he could.

I flirted, boosted his self-importance further and led him on until he believed the whole idea to interview Charlotte was his own. He coerced, twisted and bartered for a better deal, until we both got what we wanted. He let me interview his most difficult client – the one and only Charlotte Day – and I let Ray take me to bed.

It had taken weeks to set up the meeting, but at last my time had come. *It's now or never*, I thought, knowing it a cliché Jackie would not have allowed, but I no longer cared. By now, I had ideas of my own.

I turned on my brightest smile, determined to be my most charming self.

The tall, graceful woman who answered my knock wore her grey hair scraped back and twisted into a careless topknot. Stray strands stuck out at odd angles, which gave her a devil-may-care appearance. Her unusual green eyes were intelligent, but weariness etched deep lines on her face.

I knew the moment I met Charlotte Day my life was about to change.

Charlotte

February

I was supposed to be working, but in reality I sat staring out the window. The late summer sun shone on the water lapping the beach, the tuis sang in the nearby kowhai tree and the air wafting through the open windows carried a tang of seaweed and the sweet smell of roses.

A knock on the door interrupted my thoughts as I sat at the computer pretending to write the next chapter of my latest book, wondering if I cared. My long-time friend and tireless editor, Michael, was screaming in my ear to keep at it, but somehow I couldn't find the right words to create the flow needed. Dear Michael, he'd stuck by me for many years, through the good times and the bad. Since he retired, he's become my beta-reader and proofreader, but he couldn't quite let go of his lifetime role as my personal taskmaster.

I shoved my roller chair back from the desk, swung around and got to my feet, muttering under my breath about inconsiderate people arriving without an appointment. But having ignored the doorbell once when Michael called unexpectedly, I didn't want a repeat of that fiasco. Poor man spent hours looking for me.

I confronted the caller with the realisation I'd not bothered to dress well. Not feeling my best when I got up, I'd simply pulled on a comfortable pair of jeans, a loose purple top and my slippers. At least I'd brushed my thin hair into some semblance of tidy, knotting it at the back, but it was hardly done, and without any make-up, I would look very much the ageing woman I was.

The slimly built, smartly attired girl smiling at me from the step looked no more than a kid but was probably in her late twenties. Her fair hair and make-up were impeccable. I felt even older and tireder than before.

"Miss Day?" she asked.

"Yes. And you are?"

"I'm Emma. Emma Wade."

The name meant nothing to me. I looked at her blankly.

"Didn't Mr Morris tell you I was coming?"

Suddenly, my memory sparked into life. "Oh, my goodness. Is it today?"

My manager-cum-publicist, agent and oft-times provocateur, Ray Morris, had insisted I needed to do a series of interviews for a publicity story. *Needed,* he'd emphasised – and here was the girl he had entrusted with the job. *Good luck to her.* I'd argued with him at length but finally gave in. It might benefit me in the long run.

"You'd better come in, then." I opened the door wider and started to walk down the corridor, trusting the girl to follow me. "Sorry. I had completely forgotten."

I led her to my desk, sat in my chair and left her with the upright seat tucked in the corner. With the window behind me, she would only see my silhouette, which suited me fine.

"Now, Miss ... er ... what's your name again?"

"Emma Wade. Just call me Emma."

"All right, Emma, tell me what you want and how long this will take."

Not in the slightest put out by my grumpiness, which even I recognised was undeserved, the girl put her briefcase on the floor. She opened it up, showing a new journal with an intriguing cover, some folders, newspaper cuttings and sheaves of paper. I could see my name at the top of one of them.

"I'm so pleased to meet you at last, Miss Day. I have been a fan of yours for many years."

Charming too, it seemed. Or a liar, I thought, still not giving an inch.

Choosing a pen from the array on the lid of the case, she picked up the journal and sat upright. When she smiled, her whole face and eyes lit up. "I was so excited when Mr Morris commissioned me for this job. I can't tell you how much the task ahead pleases me."

"Yes, yes, but that doesn't answer my question. How long do you need? I'm busy and haven't time for this nonsense."

Still smiling, she crossed her slim, bronzed legs shod with expensive red court shoes. She leant towards me slightly, in an almost conspiratorial pose, and lowered her voice. "Mr Morris did warn me that this was his choice not yours and that I shouldn't let you put me off, never mind how much you tried. But to answer your question, I'll work in to suit you."

I sat listening to Emma with increasing dread as she explained how much time she would need and how many interviews she expected. She outlined a time frame for the research and when she hoped to have the first draft ready. It would take months.

We argued back and forth for some time over how we would go about dissecting my life and how she would assemble it again. The girl obviously thought she was writing my life story. We couldn't even agree on a starting date.

"Hold on a minute. I thought this was a series of articles about my books – not my life!"

"Well, it did start out that way," she admitted. "But the more Ray and I discussed it, the clearer it became that your story deserved a lot more attention. That's when he started talking about a book deal."

"What! How dare he; the conniving old sod!" Now I knew why Ray thought all this fuss necessary, the greedy, money-grabbing creep. *I must get rid of him.* "Wait until I have a piece of him. I do not want people poking around in my personal life. Got it?"

Studying her in the light from the window, I could see she was older than I first thought, a woman in her early thirties at least. I silently cursed Ray for getting me into this as she outlined her background: starting as a junior journalist and working her way up through senior journalist to an assistant editor with a well-known magazine before she'd turned freelance.

What had happened to make her change direction, I wondered, seeing how sadness ringed her eyes. What heartbreak had halted her in her tracks? Maybe I had a germ of an idea for another book.

"Mr Morris tells me it's your decision whether I put your anecdotes together my way from the facts I know – and can find out – and what I can surmise about bits in between. Or we can write your life story together." She paused. "I do know something of your past, having already done some research, but only you can put it into context."

Anecdotes! My life was more than anecdotes! But I didn't trust Ray's intentions and decided to put her off. "How can you know anything about me, other than my work?" I demanded, indignant, and scared to think what knowledge she might have. "I never talk about my personal life."

A slow smile spread across her face, her eyes hooded. "I still have friends and contacts in the right places. I know how to open drawers and files."

Despite her winning smile, I felt a lump settle in my stomach at the thought of what I had got myself into.

Taking stock of the conversation, Emma tried a different approach. "I understand from Ray that you will be the credited author of your autobiography, but he doesn't believe you have the time nor the ... um, shall we say, inclination, to write it without my help."

This young woman was clever. I was not at all inclined to write anything about myself. That's why

I'd become an author in the first place, so I could escape to other worlds of my own making.

"That'd be right," I muttered. "What makes you think you can?" Even to my ear that sounded nasty, but I wasn't ready to concede defeat, even if it wasn't her I was doing battle with.

"Inner knowledge," she replied with a slow smile. Looking me in the eye, she threw my words from an earlier article back at me, quoting: "Self-discipline, innate ability and determination."

Bitch! Not only charming but smart and cunning to boot. I could get to like this woman. I snorted in acknowledgement and saw her shoulders relax a little.

"I took on this commission because of the challenge and the opportunity to write a good story. I believe it will be a great story if you are willing to help."

Maybe she had a point. "Ray has done a real hard sell on you, I can tell." For the first time, I had some sympathy for this fellow pawn in front of me. "Just like he's done to me really. Neither of us has any option here. You have been sent to write my story. If you fail, he will make your life hell; if I make it difficult for you, he will make my life hell. How on earth does he get away with it?"

My rhetorical question hung in the air.

"Is there anything I can do to make this easier for you? I don't want to put you in an embarrassing or delicate position." Emma seemed genuinely concerned at my reticence.

With a sigh, I decided to accept the overture with the grace it was offered. "Coffee?"

"Yes, please."

Rising carefully to ease the pain, I indicated she should follow me to the kitchen. She chatted while I made the coffee – strong and black – the way I liked it. Gone were the days when a frothy, milky coffee was my favourite. I could no longer be bothered making sure I had milk in the house, and I hated that long-life stuff. I handed her a mug of steaming black liquid, waiting for the expression of disgust I was normally greeted with.

Instead, her eyes lit up. "Thank you. Just the way I like it."

Another thing to like about her; maybe she would grow on me.

"Sorry, what were you saying?" I asked.

"I suggested we could start today, since I'm here and you don't appear busy right now."

I glanced at the clock on the wall. I'd been at my desk since seven, and here it was ten-thirty already. In that time, I'd hardly managed to string two words together that I liked, and my mind had long since wandered from the task in hand. The nagging pain in my side was dragging me down.

"I'll give you one hour. Then I'm going for a walk before my lunch and will be back at the grindstone by one."

"Excellent. Do you want to talk here or at your desk?"

I shrugged. "Here will do."

"I'll just get my notebook. Won't be a tick," she said as she fled out the door.

I pulled out a chair and sat at the kitchen table,

nervously adjusting the ill-assorted bunch of garden flowers I'd picked and jammed into a vase yesterday. She could only write what I told her, but I couldn't help feeling afraid she would see I was hiding things and get too nosy. Lost in thought as I gazed across the garden, I hardly noticed she'd returned and had taken up the seat to my right, at the end of the table, coffee in one hand and pen poised.

"Penny for them?" she interrupted.

"Hmm? Oh, them, hardly worth even that much." Rearranging myself in the chair to face her, I asked, "So where do you want to start?" My bad mood had not yet completely dissipated.

"We could start with the first thought that comes to mind or – my preference – we could start at the beginning." She pulled a small Dictaphone from her pocket. "Is it okay for me to record our conversations?"

"No. It is not." I was blunt, but I didn't want her replaying every hesitation, every change of direction, listening for an uncertain tone of voice and trying to pick where I might be hiding something.

She shrugged. "Okay. I can take notes. Now, where would you like to start?"

I thought briefly about where that might be, before letting my writer's thinking get the better of me. "I was born, so my mother told me, just after midnight one bitterly cold night. It was late February, the year before war was declared, during the worst snow of the winter. Even so, it fell silently, clinging to every surface where it settled. Piling up on window sills, weighing down branches stripped bare of leaves and blocking doorways as the swirling wind tossed the flakes around in the pitch-dark sky. By morning, the snow lay in drifts as high as the second storey window. A bitter chill settled in the house ... something like that, you mean?" I asked innocently in a teasing tone.

She laughed – a hearty chuckle, her eyes shining. "I fell into that one," she said. "That, literally, was 'the beginning', but it sounded more like the beginning of one of your novels, poetic and descriptive, rather than the beginning of your life. I'm thinking of something more, um, factual."

"Oh, you want boring," I said, pretending to misunderstand.

"No. Not exactly boring, but – let's see ... I know you were born in England, so what are your earliest memories?"

That's easy, I thought, my earliest memories are linked to the things my mother cherished: crystal and silver, jewellery and fine china, and me.

In my mother's beloved china cabinet sat the silver, porcelain and crystal she'd saved for and bought, because they showed style and class. Family treasures sat alongside newer purchases. What hadn't been in the cabinet had been displayed around the house. Sometimes she would change objects around to suit an occasion or to put flowers in a vase, but jewellery was her weakness. Some of it was genuine, but as I found out later, most of it was costume jewellery. Not the cheap bling we find everywhere today, but well-crafted crystals, pearls and jets. She taught me to recognise the difference between classy and trashy – by her standards at least – and learn that all things that glittered were not diamonds to be sought after.

Necklaces, bracelets and rings filled her jewellery box. She loved large pieces, which, for such a small person was unusual, but they suited her. Two gold lockets with tiny curls of hair were locked away in the cabinet, along with a silver-edged tortoiseshell comb with its long spikes for holding a bun in place. There were other things in the cabinet too: items that appeared at strange times; items she had not bought. I didn't want to talk about the meaning behind those particular things in her cabinet, nor why I'd changed my name.

Random, unconnected memories from across the years came to mind as I sat thinking. The first was when I was nine.

*****

"Rose-Anne?" My mother never shortened my name. "What are you doing?" Her voice carried up the stairs to where I sat on the landing.

"Nothing, Mother."

"Nothing is not an answer, you must be doing something: sitting, standing, looking, touching."

"Sorry, Mother. I am sitting on the floor, looking at your things in the china cabinet."

"Then you are wasting time. Come here and help me."

"Yes, Mother." I would not dare disobey, or not answer her. She had a way of making me feel guilty if I disappointed her. I hurried down the stairs to the kitchen.

"Ah, there you are. Set the table, dear. Supper is ready, when your father gets home."

For all his charming smiles and smooth manners, my father was someone I was more than slightly afraid of. I carefully set out the knives and forks as I'd been taught: correctly spaced and straight, with the spoon beside the knife, not across the top and put the loaf of bread on the board, its knife on the table with some butter, and milk. My mother considered it working class to put a milk bottle on the table. Milk always had to be in a jug.

"I've finished. Can I watch the tell ... um, TV, please?" I would ask, careful not to say 'telly' as all my school friends did. If I shortened the name at all, I could call it a TV. Television was a rarity. After the war, broadcasts had started up again, and now two years later, more and more people were watching.

"May I," Mother corrected. "Of course you can, because you have eyes so you are able to. But you are asking permission, so the question is: May I?"

"Yes, Mother. Sorry. May I?"

The cartoons were only on in the afternoon; the news and documentaries took the evening slots, so I was hopeful.

"No. You may not. Television is for after supper. I've told you that before. Why don't you listen, girl?"

"Yes, Mother."

Disappointed I would miss out on TV again, I sat on one of the chairs, rested my chin in my hands and watched my mother stirring the soup on the Aga. As she lifted the spoon to taste it, she turned her head slightly towards me.

"Mother? What are those marks on the side of your face?"

She tensed and hid her face with her hand. Her eyes carefully avoided mine. Turning away to rinse the spoon in the sink, she said cheerily, "They're nothing ... I, ah, slipped on the steps this morning, and ..." Her voice shook. "And grazed my face on the wall." Suddenly she became brisk. "Now, have you made sure all your books and toys are put away properly, dear? You know your father gets angry if the place is not tidy. Go and check."

I slid from the chair and trudged out of the kitchen, along the hall through to the lounge, picking up a book I'd dropped. A doll sat on one chair, and another lay on the floor. I threw them into the window seat cavity. Then I settled myself on top, leaning against the window, staring out at the street beyond, and wondered why my mother would lie to me. Lying was not allowed, as I found out to my horror when she rubbed soap on my tongue the one time I had tried. Or worse, when my father thought I'd lied to him. But lie she did. I knew that with the certainty of youth. The scratches were on the wrong side of her face to have been caused by the concrete wall.

*****

Dragging my mind back from that time, I realised Emma had been watching me, patiently waiting for me to speak while all those thoughts drifted through my mind. I wondered how long it had been - obviously not too long or she would have prompted me, but long enough. I eased myself into a more comfortable position and began to tell Emma a different story.

"As an only child I learnt to entertain myself. Much of my time I spent around adults, which meant always being on my best behaviour, seen maybe, but never heard. Mostly people ignored me. I learnt to live within my head. I watched, I listened; I had imaginary friends and my doll friends to talk to when I needed them, and I tried not to attract attention."

Emma scribbled furiously. "Go on."

"I have no memory of the war years other than a few things my mother told me. Those years had no impact on my life. My father was older, so he wasn't in the forces; I don't think he even signed up for the Home Guard. Most of what I remember is into the late forties, early fifties. I'm trying to recall when rationing ended. Some of the things I associate with my childhood, like ice cream and crisps, weren't available during the war. You'll need to do your research and find out when rationing stopped, if you're going to include that rubbish."

I carried on with a few arbitrary stories, watching as she wrote, wondering just what she did know about me. A few minutes later, I decided it was her turn. "Now. I think you need to tell me what you know, and I'll fill in any details – if I choose to."

"That's hardly going to get us anywhere." Emma looked at me with a quizzical expression. "Most of what I know is in the public arena anyway."

"So, tell me," I insisted.

Emma put her pen down, leant back in the chair and, with one arm casually resting on the table, started to tell me my life history.

"Your public profiles say you were born near Thornbury in Gloucestershire. And going by what you described earlier, possibly in the middle of a winter snowstorm, which matches your February birthday. A belated Happy Birthday, by the way."

I listened as she listed two of the places I'd lived as a child, and the last school I had gone to – boring, factual stuff. And other so-called 'facts' I had invented when I turned fifteen and adopted a new name. A good researcher might be able to find out more about me if they knew my real name. I hoped she didn't.

"You were fifteen, and by then living in Bristol, when you joined an amateur musical theatre group and learnt your craft doing chorus work. You rose quickly through the ranks and became one of their leading lights when you were 'discovered'. You attended the Bristol Old Vic Theatre School. Your first role there was as a chorus girl in *Salad Days*, which then toured to London. By twenty, you had major roles in just about every production that offered. I have the list somewhere if you really want it all."

I shook my head. She continued reeling off the facts and fallacies surrounding my career, but I noticed all the things she left out too. What I wasn't sure about was whether she *really* didn't know about the missing bits or whether she hoped I'd tell her all my secrets, thinking she knew them anyway. I'd need to tread carefully.

"Do you want me to list your whole career?" Emma asked, waving some papers about.

I shrugged. "Not really. I just wanted to know

what research you'd done before you got here so I can decide whether you are any good at your job."

"Do I pass?"

"You'll do."

"There is no record of you ever doing any theatre work after 1959. No one knew why, or what had happened to you, or where you had gone." She paused, waiting for a response.

The silence lengthened.

"So, do you want to tell me why you suddenly disappeared at the age of twenty?"

I'd expected the question: it had to come sooner or later. "No. I don't."

Given the look on Emma's face, she clearly wasn't satisfied with my reply but wisely chose not to challenge me yet. The question would raise its ugly head again.

"Can we get back to your stories about when you were young, then? What got you into acting in the first place?"

"Being around so many adults I learnt to act and be what and who they wanted. I suppose that skill has held me in good stead all these years and given me the discipline to be self-contained."

"What do you mean by that?"

"Well, as an artist one has to be disciplined – able to put in the commitment. An author needs to sit at a desk and write, anything, even if it's all deleted tomorrow. You have to pour your soul into your writing if you are going to be convincing. Well, it's the same with acting. You have to become the person you are portraying. My mother, who always called me by my full name, used to tell me that shortening my name changed my identity, which is what I wanted, even if she didn't. I soon learnt that an actress could become anyone at any time, and the more often I did that, the less often I had to be just plain me."

"Fantastic," she said. "Just the sort of insight I'm looking for."

"By the time I was six, I had lived in three houses I could remember. The one where I was born; one in a village in Essex, so the family could be nearer London for some reason I never found out; and one in Cornwall. I suspect we went there to avoid the worst of the war."

I settled into my story quite quickly and without any particular qualms, which surprised me. Emma was a good listener as I jumped from memory to memory.

"My mother was never far from my side. After school she devoted her time to making sure I did my homework, or taking me for walks. She took me to ballet and singing lessons, both of which I loved. At home she constantly worked: cleaning, washing and cooking, but she loved beautiful things and dressed well.

"I remember once being told my mother had held ideas above her station her whole life. I can still hear the woman's voice: 'Her family comes from good working-class background, and she should be proud of it, not hanker after something she doesn't deserve.'

"I didn't understand her reasoning at the time, and even less now, but society was different back then. Women – and children – were expected to know their place and more often than not were kept in their place by other women."

"This is interesting stuff. You said you loved song and dance from an early age. Do you have any highlights or stories from that time?" she asked.

"I remember my mother telling me once our ballet class put on a mini-show. I'd only been a tot, maybe four, but we each held a rose and had to put them down in a row at the front of the stage, dance around and return to our own flower. Somehow I finished up at the wrong end of the line from mine, so I ran along, picked it up and took it back to the place I'd been at the other end. I think we were supposed to be in height formation, but I didn't understand that. She said the audience loved it. I suppose it would have seemed cute."

Emma had stirred up so many memories. Yet childhood memories are fragmentary, anchored by an event or picture in your head unrelated to time and place, and reliant on adults to put them in order. I used to wonder why one incident would stick in my mind while others disappeared.

Like the time I fell down the cliff. I remember it clearly. I was about eight and playing in the clifftop park overlooking the beach. The ball went over the fence, and I climbed over to get it, but the grass clippings tipped there by the lawnmower man gave way and I rolled head over heels down the cliff until a tree broke my fall. I walked away uninjured.

I'd wondered at the time why my mother was so

ill after my fall. I was the one who had fallen, not her, but she was the one who needed the doctor and rest in a dark room, taking tablets. I was more upset and frightened by that fact than by the fall. I didn't see her for days. I heard my father shouting at her, blaming her for my fall. She emerged looking pale, with purple bruises around her eyes. Not long after that, a silver cake server appeared in the china cabinet. Many years passed before I learnt the significance of one event and its connection to the other.

Or the pale blue eggs I found in the bird's nest hidden in the hedgerow I passed every day walking to and from school. I never saw any birds and the eggs never hatched. I just remember getting a thrill knowing I knew where they were hidden. It was my secret. I became very good at keeping secrets. Later, I learnt the reason the beautiful blue eggs didn't hatch was because the parents had abandoned the nest.

I can remember dozens more incidents like that – haphazard, disconnected, but each formed my childhood in their own way and, as I later discovered, they were all linked albeit in a disjointed fashion.

Not that I told Emma any memories like that, except the one about the bird's egg, which I still had with me. They were too close to the things I wanted to remain hidden.

I glanced at the clock and realised I'd talked far too long. During that time, Emma had listened, scribbling the odd note from time to time, but not once had she interrupted while I relived events as if they had happened moments before, rather than a lifetime ago.

Now she asked a few questions, trying to elicit more information before I sent her on her way.

"You've talked a lot about your mother, who was obviously a major influence in your life, far more than most mothers I would suspect. Certainly, far more than my mother ever was. Is there a reason for that, do you think?"

"Oh yes," I answered. "There were reasons, but nothing I want to tell my adoring public about. It's private. Time's up, young lady. I have to get back to work."

I would, in fact, go and lie down. I really didn't feel well.

"Of course, a deal is a deal." Emma closed her notebook and clipped her pen to it. Standing up, she extended her hand. "Thank you for your time, Miss Day."

I stood too and took her hand.

"Same time Wednesday?"

Emma

I set the GPS on my phone and wound my newly purchased Swift along the narrow road from Otitori Bay to Titirangi and through unfamiliar streets back to the city. I got lost because I wasn't paying attention to the directions and had to turn around, but once back on the main route again I had time to consider how different her lifestyle was to mine.

Her simple board and batten home, once a small bach but extended and modernised over the decades, nestled in the bush. Too deep in the bush for my central city tastes, but if the houses I passed were anything to go by, she wasn't the only one who liked seclusion. It would have been a long way out in the sixties when she first came here. It wasn't easy to find now. Had she come to hide?

I noticed she would cock her head every now and then to listen when a bird sang or when the distinctive sound of the kereru's wings flying past drifted in through the open window. I had never taken notice of those things before. City life doesn't lend itself to such time wasting, but she often just sat and stared outside with a look of great contentment – either towards the bay below or at the trees. I was almost jealous.

I drove away from Charlotte Day's home feeling pleased. The first interview had gone well, and I think she may even have liked me a little. In some ways she surprised me, talking so easily about her mother, but I think she was trying to hide much of her past by telling me more general things. I decided to forgive her for now. I'd not been honest with her either. There were things I wanted to know, but I could wait. Meanwhile, I pretended to enjoy listening to stories of her early childhood and those of her mother.

I'd never given a moment's thought to history of any kind. I like the here and now. I like this modern world where things happen fast. Today's news focuses on the now events: what's happening where and to whom. The magazine world spotlights today's fashions, today's celebrities and tomorrow's possibilities. No one in the industry wanted to know about the past. I briefly wondered why Jackie had sent me on this mission. She'd never wanted to write articles about faded celebs before. Why now? Buried deep in my own troubles, I didn't give it much thought.

I was mildly curious as to why Charlotte had vanished completely from the London stage, only to reappear in New Zealand years later. Her stage career was short and ended abruptly while she was still young.

I thought about all the questions I'd need to ask. Where had her mother grown up? When did they move to Bristol? Who had she trained with? Possible celebs she once knew. Simple stuff to make her feel safe until I could ask the more searching questions about family, about relationships – about why she'd left the stage. I'd even talk about her damned books. NOTE TO SELF: Pick up some copies to read. Anything, until I could ask her about that blasted photo Jackie had given me. Where had I seen it before? I'd not noticed the original on display anywhere in Charlotte's home, and I didn't even know if it was of her or just a publicity shot used as a teaser. But then why would someone use a photo of a child taken eighty or ninety years ago as a publicity photo?

Eventually, my thoughts turned to Ray and how a relationship of sorts had developed between us. I did not trust him one bit but would tolerate him for now while I got the stories I wanted. I found myself getting tangled between what I was prepared to let on to Ray and the truth.

"So tell me about yourself," he'd asked the first time we'd met. "What brought a Wellington girl to Auckland?"

"I felt like a change of scenery and a chance to try my hand at some freelance journalism," I bluffed.

"Are you married?"

"No. No ties, just carefree me."

The truth was more painful. I had no one. I never knew my father; I'd left my husband and lost my baby. Now my mother was gone, too. Ray wouldn't have wanted to know about any of it. He was far more interested in talking about himself – and name-dropping.

I'd rented a fully furnished flat in Mt Eden and since then Ray had got into the habit of calling in after work for a drink and a chat. I was a good listener, he said, which meant I didn't interrupt. I wasn't interested in his boasting.

"So how did you get on?" He strode past me as I opened the door, went straight to the cabinet and poured a glass of bourbon.

"Good, for a first meeting."

"Did the old witch give you any trouble?"

He threw back the golden liquor and refilled his glass. I groaned inwardly. It looked like he was settling in for a long night. I wasn't in the mood. The sex was good, even great at times. It felt nice to be wanted and fussed over after such a long time, but my rising level of guilt made me anxious. I'd hated watching my mother use people, yet here I was doing the same thing – telling *him* one thing and Charlotte another to get what I wanted.

"No. Why would she?"

"She can be a right old battle-axe when she wants to be. Stubborn, bossy and downright contrary."

"You mean she doesn't always do as you tell her." I almost laughed in his face but thought better of it. I didn't want to get on the wrong side of Ray. "Or maybe she just doesn't like men."

Ray shrugged. "Hadn't thought of it that way ... Yes. Could be ... She's always been single as far as I know. She's very pally with that Michael Grainger, though. Gives him more than the time of day, I can tell you that for a fact."

Fixing myself a glass of wine, I stored that piece of

information away to be followed up later. Ray's hint there could be more between Charlotte and Michael would be worth looking into.

"Tell me what sort of day you've had," I said, knowing he would instantly forget any further questions about my interview with Charlotte, and hoping he wouldn't stay long. I wanted to work on the stories she had told me.

He moved closer, took my chin in his hand and kissed me.

"I've had a great day. And I can think of the perfect way to end it."

Charlotte

Early March

True to her word, Emma didn't contact me again until the following Wednesday. In the interim, Michael had been mollified by some new words filling up a few more chapters, but I knew many of those would get deleted and rewritten when I edited the final draft, and so did he.

She turned up on my doorstep at the allotted time, still immaculate. Her fair hair cut in a bob framed her face perfectly, and her make-up was subtle and soft, but I detected a hard core that belied her image.

I made coffee, and we took our mugs into the lounge. On that beautiful late summer day, I had thrown open the French doors overlooking the garden and pulled the chairs forward to enjoy the view of the bush and the beach below. I had even made an effort to dress nicely today, brushing my hair into a neat bun and applying some lip gloss. I wondered why I was doing so even as I did it, but I felt better for it.

Throughout the house, notebooks filled with

the nub of an idea lay forgotten where I'd left them cluttering tabletops, bookshelves and even chairs. Others, with ill-formed ideas left to fester and grow if they could, lay nearer to hand here in the living area. Pens sat beside them so I could jot down thoughts as they came to mind. I had dozens of them, with a story in every book and not enough years left in which to use them, but I was content.

My house in Titirangi was my hidey-hole. I rarely went out any more if I could avoid it. I didn't need clothes, or ornaments, or any of the modern rubbish – waste wrapped in more waste. My home was filled with all the things I liked and needed. A television, when I chose to watch it. My show music to listen to when I felt nostalgic, which had become increasingly rare – until Emma started asking questions.

I preferred my make-believe worlds. I had my books, shelves and shelves of them to read and reread as the mood took me. Every day I trod my path down to the beach where I walked, thinking, moving words around in my mind until they formed into something interesting. I had my garden and my beautiful roses, which I could deadhead when I needed to move a different set of words about. The local man came in and did the hard work: mowing lawns, trimming hedges and mulching.

My needs were simple.

"Have you thought any more about your early life since our talk last week?" Emma asked, looking at a notebook and fingering its leather cover. She sounded innocent, but I thought her a cunning little minx. She knew very well I would do everything I could to avoid thinking about the past, and fail.

"Why would I?" I asked, contrarily.

Emma simply smiled. "Because I asked you to."

Of course I had. And she knew it. The question I kept asking myself was how much could I tell her.

I settled on a safe subject.

"My hair was fine, straight and an ordinary brown with nothing much to recommend it, other than it was very long. My mother brushed it through for a hundred strokes every night without fail, plaiting it into a long, thick braid for sleeping. That way it would start off without tangles in the morning, and the waves from the plait gave it more body."

Emma raised her eyebrow, challenging me to give her something more interesting. I remembered too well, if the truth were told. It was during those times my mother would tell me her stories. Times when a dreamy look would cross her face and she would stare into the beyond, not seeing the real world in front of her. I learnt to recognise that look and keep very still and quiet. Sometimes she would absentmindedly run her hand through my hair or gently stroke my back while she talked. Those were the times I could ask questions. Other times she would lecture me in her stern voice.

I just needed to carefully choose the stories suitable for Emma's ears.

*****

"Please tell me the story about that little glass trinket box," I asked Mother one evening before bed, pointing through the door of the closed china cabinet. I knew where the key was kept, but I would never open it without permission. I feared the consequences.

"That once belonged to my Granny Davies, my father's mother, who came to live with us when I was only a few years older than you are now."

She took the key from its resting place in the jug adorning the top of the cabinet and opened the door. Lifting the small, cut-glass box with its silver lid she laid it in my open palms. I felt honoured to be trusted to hold such a beautiful thing.

"It's not worth anything. It's just glass and silver plate, but it has sentimental value because it reminds me of Granny every time I see it. There is more to things than what they cost. It's what they represent that is important. Don't ever forget that." She took the box from me and replaced it in the cabinet, locking the door behind her.

"Bath time," she said. It seemed I would have to wait until next time to find out more about her granny.

Our routine never varied. Every night she would run my bath, checking the water was not too hot, and sit on the side of it, watching me, as if afraid to let me out of her sight. Then she would pull up the chair in my room while I sat on the stool at her feet so she could brush my hair the obligatory hundred strokes.

As she brushed, she talked. "I loved my Granny."

I was so happy she was going to continue her story I almost said something but held back just in time. If I let her talk, she would say more than if I asked questions.

"I was her favourite. She would always sneak a treat for me, especially if my mother had been hard on me again. Mother was very harsh sometimes, but my papa and my granny made up for it. I was heartbroken when she died, but she'd had a hard life, had Granny."

Countless brush strokes were pulled through my hair in silence.

Suddenly she stopped brushing and stared into the distance through walls as thick as the years were long.

"Granny gave me a wide belt once. Its links were made of beaten silver. It was the most beautiful thing I had ever seen. Only eighteen and a half inches long – the size her waist had been when she was young. I must have been about sixteen or seventeen. It almost fitted me, but it wouldn't quite do up. My mother took it away and I never saw it again. I wonder where it is now." She sighed, and continued brushing.

"Granny was a cheery soul, but she seemed an old woman to me at the time she came to live with us. The once tiny girl who could fit such a wonderful belt had become a plump lady with several chins and feet that bulged over the sides of her shoes. She was a great cook, and the kitchen became her domain, but she was old and got sick. Only a few years later she looked like a shrivelled sparrow, with deep lines etched on her face and sad eyes."

In an instant, putting the brush to one side, she wiped her eyes with her hands. "Enough. Bed now," and with a kiss on my forehead, she was gone, the light out and the door shut.

*****

"What a lovely story," said Emma, jotting down notes. "How old were you when you heard it?"

"Maybe seven."

"So, roughly what year did your mother's ... um ... grandmother go to live with the family?" she asked.

"Must have been late twenties, I think. More or less. Back then it was normal."

What I didn't tell Emma was how, when Mother felt happy, she would smile slowly, her face going soft as she thought about what the item meant to her. Or when, at other times, her face muscles tightening, she would refuse to tell me its story – usually after a night when I'd heard angry voices coming from downstairs, or woke to hear her sobbing in the room next to mine.

In the dark, before sleep overtook me, I liked to dream about the things I wanted in life: to be beautiful, to be loved, to have a sister – or someone to talk to – and wishing my parents wouldn't fight so much. But they were only dreams, as I was yet to discover.

After a string of loud arguments between my parents, we moved.

My mother cried a lot.

One day I heard her shout, "You'll live to regret what you've done, you bastard."

I didn't know what she meant.

I couldn't tell Emma about those memories. But what I could tell her about, I decided, was the lasting memory of the move to my second home.

*****

"I was five and had just started school. We were made to do our PE lessons outside. I hated every minute of it. Dressed only in baggy bloomers and woollen singlets, so we would have dry clothes and shoes to get back into, we had to run around the playground every day, regardless of the weather.

"The freshly fallen snow lay soft and undisturbed on the frozen ground. The quiet of a snowy landscape remarkable and its beauty breathtaking, until people and vehicles churn it up into slush: grey, watery and icy. In that frosty world, my feet became red and sore, my whole body aching with the cold until I fell ill.

"It seemed like forever that I lay in a darkened room. Mother told me later it was many long weeks. The doctors worried I had caught the poliovirus, but nothing ever came of it, and I escaped the misery of the iron lung some poor victims had to endure.

"Running around in the cold had nothing to do with it, of course. So whether I had really picked up the poliovirus or had a bad case of flu or pneumonia, I'll never know. We didn't stay there long."

"What's an iron lung?" Emma asked.

"Goodness, girl. Don't you know? It was a fearsome machine. Back in the forties and fifties, the virus could either paralyse the lungs or the legs. Too many people found themselves stuck inside the lung machine for hours on end with only their head sticking out, or else struggling to walk with crutches and iron frame callipers on their legs. Search on the Internet for it, if you want to know more, or better still, visit MOTAT. There's one on display there, I think.

"Anyway, that's all for today, Emma." I stood up and picked up the coffee mugs. "I really must get on. I'm finding this whole thing disruptive, and I need to concentrate on my make-believe worlds – the ones that pay the bills – rather than anything past and done for."

She agreed, but with less enthusiasm. "I'd like to come to see you more often if you don't mind. Please? It's awfully frustrating not being able to structure the story as a whole. I need a much larger picture before I can start."

I had some sympathy with her plight, understanding how authors worked.

"I'll come any time of the day or night to suit you," she begged.

Needing time to think about her request, I head towards the kitchen with the mugs in my hand. Emma turned to follow.

"Is that your mother's china cabinet?"

The bow-fronted cabinet stood against the wall behind where she'd been sitting.

"Yes." I called from the kitchen.

Emma kept firing questions at me about what she could see. I had no choice but to stand behind her and explain each item. The silver-backed hairbrush my mother always used, her hand mirror, the cake server my mother refused to use, a small pale blue bird's egg and a silver-topped glass trinket box.

"These are all the things you talked about." Her voice sounded dazzled, as if I'd made them all up.

"Yes, they are."

"If you have a story about every item in this cabinet, I'm going to have to visit you every day for a year."

My smile slipped, feeling crooked on my face.

I looked at her imploring gaze and decided to give her one more story, but then she had to go. I'd think about whether I wanted her to visit more often later.

*****

In our new life, my mother made Cornish clotted cream by hand at least twice or three times a week, depending on how many people came to visit. In the mornings, she would pour the rich, creamy top from the milk bottles delivered to our door into a large, flat pan. The pan was put aside in the scullery to settle.

"See here, how this is done," she explained as she worked. "It's important that the cream settles and the fat comes to the top. It's got to be heated very slowly on the lowest flame until it starts to thicken around the edges. Never let it bubble. Never. That will ruin it, and you'll have to throw it out and start again."

My mouth watered as I watched. If I was lucky, she would give me scones or pikelets with jam and lashings of her home-made cream.

"Not today, sweetheart. It won't be ready. Maybe tomorrow."

"Mother," I said one day as I watched the slow process of turning milk to cream. "There's a new locket in your cabinet with a picture of a man."

"You have a quick eye. I only just put it in there yesterday."

"I know, with the silver cup with the W on it. I like looking at your things. Who is it?"

"That's my father. My Papa. And the cup belonged to him." Tears prickled her eyes, and she wiped them away quickly. "Don't you remember him?"

"Was he the man who used to sit in the chair with blankets wrapped around him in the room with glass walls? It doesn't look like him. I remember him. He was thin, with bits of white, fluffy hair sticking up and long hair on his lip. I liked his blue eyes."

"Yes. That was Papa. And yes, he had very kind eyes, did my Papa. The photo of him in the locket was taken when he was much younger. Papa was very ill towards the end when you knew him. Do you remember the house at all?"

"I don't think so," I said, biting my lip while I thought hard about what she'd asked. "The glass-walled room looking out over the garden. The strawberries and daffodils."

"Clever girl. What else do you remember?"

"Um. Dark stairs going straight up, I always thought the bogeyman would get me if I went up them. And across the yard, a big table in a dark room with two big lights hanging low over it. I remember being too small to see over the top. I played with the balls in the little nets on the corners. Where was that?"

My mother had gone very quiet, and her face paled. She sat down slowly on the chair opposite me, drying her hands on a tea towel. I waited.

"It was the billiard room in the garage. I never knew you'd been in there," was all she said.

*****

By the time I'd finished, Emma had added several more pages to her notes.

"Long before homogenised milk was ever heard of, we used to get old-fashioned full-cream milk in pint and half-pint bottles delivered to the door. Cream came in quarter-pint bottles. It was nowhere near as good as Mother's traditional hand-made clotted cream but far better than the creams you can buy these days."

"Is that the long-handled spoon she used?" She pointed to the cabinet and the silver-plate, round-headed, flat spoon with holes.

"Yes, it is. I can still remember its unique taste. A thick, rich, faintly sweet, buttery mixture, with a nutty aroma that came from the ever-so-gentle cooking. My mother also made her own special clotted cream fudge and home-made ice cream."

"Sounds yum. And the silver cup and locket on the next shelf. Were they your grandfather's?"

Again, I nodded. I kept everything. In this throwaway world with its plastic dependence and need to buy everything bright and shiny new, I sometimes wonder what history will say of this era. The young just don't seem to appreciate the past enough. But then, neither did I, when I was young.

Emma

I began to enjoy the bush as I drove back and forth between her place and mine. The magnificent nikaus and ferns, in particular, caught my eye amongst the backdrop of dark green, and I saw so many native birds, now I knew what to look for, more than I'd ever seen in the city. I'd even taken to driving to some of the other bays in the area, up and down the narrow, winding roads, most of which Charlotte said were unsealed in the early days, leading to hidden coves she'd told me about. Many a time, I would park and walk along the seashore, gazing up at the steep cliffs, or sit and listen to the sounds of the water.

"Everything is too fast, these days," she'd moaned. "Everyone rushing here, there and everywhere just to get wherever five minutes earlier. No one takes time to appreciate what's around them any more."

I could see what she meant and began to understand why Charlotte could feel at peace in a place like this. I'd started to notice all sorts of things I'd never noticed before, but mostly, these walks gave me time to think. I ticked off in my mind what I'd achieved.

I am definitely winning her over. She's let me back sooner than planned, so that's a good sign, but she still insists on me calling her Miss Day. I've got to break that barrier down somehow.

There's a lack of personal photos around the house. Most women I know of, and older women especially, have loads of photos about the place.

The black-and-white photo of the child in the promotional shot is definitely not on display in her office or living room. I didn't manage to sneak into her bedroom, but that's the last place I'd expect to see it. I need to figure out how I can ask for its story.

Charlotte is proving a far more interesting subject than I first thought.

She still talks a lot about her mother and her young life, but I want to move on beyond that time.

Potential problem: I'll need to write something. She's bound to ask to see a draft copy sooner or later. She's too clever to let that pass. Damn and blast the woman! But first, I have to make sense of everything. I have to understand who she really is.

Maybe I should write her life story after all. I hadn't intended to, even though that is what I told her – and what Ray thinks. All I wanted to do was worm my way in to find some juicy gossip – maybe something to do with why she disappeared all those years ago, like Jackie had asked for, and be on my way, but nothing so far. If I'm clever, I could use what I find as leverage, and *I* might be able to make money from it one day, instead of Ray. That would be a bonus.

I just need to find an excuse to get inside the cabinet and have a good look.

I pulled my mind back to the present and made my way home. I was sure to find Ray, if not waiting for me, at least turning up before long. I turned on the radio and started singing along to the tunes, feeling happier than I had in a long time.

Charlotte

March

I was getting suspicious by the time Emma returned for her third visit. All this delving into my past and getting me to remember the stories my mother told would have little impact on the biography she professed to be writing. Why did she want to know about events that happened so long ago? I might find history fascinating, but I doubted it would make interesting reading in a biography and certainly not for any journalistic articles about my books, if they ever see the light of day.

The images of life over the last century or so that I'd given her would hardly improve the personal story she was seeking. If she thought she could fool me and lull me into a false sense of complacency and I'd let something slip, she had another think coming. Two could play at that game. She was getting nothing that couldn't have happened to anyone else of my grandmother's, mother's or my era.

Much to my surprise, I began to enjoy reliving

some of those moments. Others, not so. Some I tried to forget or at least skip over, remembering only the good times.

"Thank you for letting me come back so soon," Emma said, settling into the cane two-seater opposite me.

"The sooner we get this over with, the better," I growled.

I didn't want to let on that it suited me. My current work-in-progress had stalled. No, worse than that, I'd hit a brick wall. The story no longer resonated with me, and I'd lost patience with it. I didn't need to write anything to keep bread on the table, I did it because a story needed writing. When a story ended up going nowhere, I'd reached the point in my life when I could afford to ditch it and try something new.

That something new sat in front of me: I was intrigued by this girl. I knew nothing about her, but I suspected there was more to her than met the eye. I'd already invented half a story but I needed to know something about her to make it matter. I just had to work out how I could play gamekeeper and poacher at the same time, interviewer and interviewee.

"So, tell me, what time of the year did you love the most?" she asked.

"Easy," I answered instantly. "Summer: always has been, always will be. Sunshine restores the energy lost through a dark, cold winter."

And that grey time when one never knew the mood of the house from one day to another, I thought, but didn't voice.

"One summer, we rented a beach hut; one of the lucky ones, I was told. I loved the beach, still do. My mother and I would go there every afternoon after school. We would get changed in the hut and hang up our clothes. Then she would pull out her striped deckchair with its footrest, put on her sunglasses, coat her body with coconut oil and bathe in the sun. I was free to play."

Over the years, the beach became my sanctuary. The place I felt most at peace. It still is.

*****

"Can I play in the rock pools over there, please, Mother?"

"Yes, dear, but put your sandals on first."

"Aw. Do I have to?" I hated those plastic sandals.

"Yes, you do, or else you sit here beside me and don't move. It's your choice."

Not much of a choice, I thought, as the rock pools beckoned. I obediently put on my plastic sandals, picked up my bucket and went exploring.

I ran along the beach feeling the sand getting caught between my toes and under the straps and rubbing up and down until my skin was raw. When I got to the rock pools, I washed my feet in the first one I came to. One day, things didn't work out so well. I'd hardly taken two steps before I slipped over as my feet slid around inside the sandals.

I checked my mother wasn't looking and took them off. I liked being in bare feet. There was one special pool that was long enough and deep enough to lie in. I stepped down onto the sandy bottom and felt a sharp pain. I could see blood colouring the water.

I screamed. "Mummy!" forgetting she liked to be called Mother.

People started running towards me, and I was lifted out. My mother arrived soon after, breathless.

"There there, dear. Don't be frightened." She wrapped my foot up in a towel someone had given her. "It's only a small cut. It just looks worse because of the blood in the water."

A strange man carried me back to the hut, but I don't remember what happened after that. What I did remember, though, was a new feeling. Somewhere in the back of my mind lingered the thought that even the happiest of places can have a dark side. That feeling shaped my life.

The next time we came to the beach the hated plastic sandals were new ones.

"Now. Listen carefully," said my mother as she strapped them on tightly. "Do not take these off. Not for any reason. Do you hear me? If you take them off again, I will not bring you to the beach with me. You can stay home with your father."

I accepted my fate. I couldn't stay home with my father by myself.

I put on the sandals and headed to the rock pools, searching under loose rocks for crabs or tiny shrimp, or to watch how the sea anemone would close up as soon as something came too close. I swam in the larger pools, collected shells and soaked up the sounds and smells of the seashore. I loved the beach. It was my haven: a peaceful, carefree place, where all sat well in my world.

*****

"So, what were two of the occasions you enjoyed most?" Emma asked, pushing her agenda.

"May Day: on the first of May, heralding the coming summer and celebrated with parades, dancing around the maypole, in and out with the ribbons, and crowning the May Queen. And Christmas. I loved Christmas: the fire burning in the hearth, the carol singing in the streets and the smell of roast chicken, a rarity in those days.

"Christmas pudding with custard and brandy sauce, complete with the hidden sixpences that somehow always ended up in my serving. I loved the decorations, making paper chains from crêpe paper and the lights on the tree. And I especially loved seeing all the people coming to the house parties: my own private fairyland."

"Go on," urged Emma. "I've never had a winter Christmas."

"My mother would spend the day in the kitchen preparing the food. I never knew what most of it was called, and I was certainly never allowed any, but I could watch. She would then get dressed in one of her sparkly gowns with silver or gold threads, put on a crystal necklace or jet beads, or whatever jewellery looked best, brush her nearly black hair until it shone and push it into waves around her face; and the final touch, her red lipstick."

I left out any references to my father other than in general terms, even though he was as much a presence on these occasions as my mother. He would get dressed up in a dinner jacket and cravat; it looked so different to his usual open-neck shirt and waistcoat. Not that I saw much of my father. He was always a shadowy figure in the background of my life, but someone I instinctively knew could instil fear into my mother. If Emma wondered why I never mentioned my father, she didn't voice her thoughts.

"The best night was Christmas Eve. I used to sit on the stairs, looking through the banister rails, watching the people arriving, creeping lower and lower, careful not to be seen and get sent back to bed. The women wore gowns in many colours, the men in black jackets and bow ties."

My father was always full of good humour on nights like that, his voice smooth and cheery. He would kiss the women in welcome, touching their shoulders or putting his hand on the small of their back – or lower – laughing and flirting with them.

"The fur wraps used to be draped over the banister. I loved to stroke the soft fur if I could creep near enough without being seen. My mother always knew I was there and would let me stay up, but lo and behold if my father caught me. Later I would fall asleep to the sounds of conversation and laughter, knowing that the next day was Christmas Day."

"Were things really that formal? Even in private homes?"

"Yes, they were, in our part of England anyway. People dressed for special occasions. This was after the war, and everyone wanted it to get back to something like it was before. We'd gone to Cornwall because it was considered safer. Not that I knew that at the time, of course. Later, I realised my parents had more than enough money to be comfortable. They would have been considered middle class, back then. But what about you, Emma. Do you have any favourite moments or memories?"

"Some." She shrugged. "Not many. My mother and I moved around a lot so I didn't have lots of friends."

Another snippet to add to my book of words. "Really? That's a pity. Friends are important. So tell me one of your best moments."

"Ah, probably picnics. My mother liked picnics."

She didn't expand any further, so I stored the information as we chatted. She asked simple things about the places I remembered, the streets, the houses, colours, what the school looked like, did I play an instrument as well as sing in the choir and a myriad of similar questions. I hoped they were adding to the sort of picture she was creating, but I had this nagging feeling she wanted something different.

*****

The next day I heard a knock on the door, although I wasn't expecting anyone, not even Emma. I wiped my hands on the towel as I hurried to open the door.

I was stunned to see Michael. What was he doing here? It must be important if he's come unannounced.

"Hello, Lottie dear." He stepped into the hallway, kissed my cheek and walked on through. While this behaviour wasn't unusual, I wondered why he had come today.

I followed him.

"Well, hello to you too, Michael. To what do I owe the pleasure?" I waved the coffee plunger at him. Receiving a nod of approval, I filled the kettle and busied myself in the kitchen. Michael liked his coffee half-strength with milk and sugar. I checked I had both, relieved that, for once, I did.

"Do I need an excuse?" Michael asked as he sat in one of the two comfy armchairs I kept by the old range in the sitting room. My winter nook – my snug I called it, but I don't often sit there in summer. I used to light the coal range a lot and keep the kettle boiling or make soup, but it got too much for me to clean and get firewood. Now my cosy snug boasts a modern heat pump. I don't like them as much, but beggars can't be choosers, and I can't stand being cold. I only light the range these days when I need the extra comfort, when the pain settles in, and I can get my garden man to reset it for me.

"No, of course not. You're welcome any time, you know that, but you usually do have a reason, especially if you come unexpectedly," I replied pointedly, wanting an explanation.

He didn't take the bait.

I studied him fondly while waiting for the jug to boil. His large glasses with black rims sat well on his broad face, and he wore his pure white hair neatly cut short back and sides. His lanky frame looked relaxed, but he had lost weight again and was showing his age …

I first met Michael nearly fifty years ago, in the late sixties. The editor of the publishing house who had taken on my first book decided I needed one person to liaise with. Michael was the up-and-coming golden boy determined to become editor-in-chief one day, which he later achieved. He kept up with the many changes and moved from house to house when mergers and takeovers altered the whole industry.

We hit it off from day one. Michael took a real interest in my work. Every once in a while, I would turn up with my next offering, back in those heady days when publishing and selling a book was relatively easy. He helped me fix whatever problems the current book on offer had, and prepared it for publication.

We became friends as well as colleagues. He'd often invite me to spend time with his family since I had no one in New Zealand. His wife Kate took me to her heart and was the first, best and only woman friend I'd ever had.

Michael and Kate adored each other and raised a daughter and three sons. Luke, their youngest by a long way, was my favourite. I never told anyone, but I loved him from the day he was born and he was the only one I would have stay with me. He was the most like Michael in every way and, again, the only one to follow his father into the book industry. In time, he became my co-conspirator.

When Kate passed away several years ago, Michael could not be comforted. He more or less gave up on life. He stopped travelling, stopped going to the theatre, stopped everything he and Kate had done together. He even avoided book fairs and writing events. He lived quietly in the same house they'd lived in for decades, pottering in the garden, going for walks and writing his memoirs, he said. I never believed him. No one had seen a written word from him in years. He only ventured out when family forced him, or when he decided he needed to talk to me – like today ...

I handed him his coffee and pulled up my ancient captain's chair opposite him. "So," I asked again, "what does bring you here today?"

"Ray Morris."

Michael had never liked Ray. The feeling was mutual. Michael had been too old and set in his ways by the time the recession, at the turn of the century, led to the collapse of bookstores and the rise of ebooks and independent publishing. He didn't want to adapt to the modern trends in publishing and left it to the younger ones. Ray was everything Michael was not: pushy, flamboyant and self-opinionated.

"Oh, yes? Can't say he's my favourite character right now, either," I commented carefully, "but what's your problem with him this time?"

"He rang me to tell me how clever he is getting some girl journalist to do a piece on you. I don't like it. I don't like his approach, and I don't see why you have to do it at all."

Michael was never one to pull punches. He was always upfront and had always told me what he thought were my best options. He couldn't break the habit.

"Neither did I. But Ray reckons publicity about me will raise the profile of my books. And you were the one to say I needed to look at other options to sell them."

He sipped his coffee while he looked at me, weighing up his next words.

"And I stick by that," he said. "But you don't need someone like that pushing you down the path towards an exposé. It goes against everything you've done to protect yourself."

Michael – and Luke, if I was honest – were the only ones who knew everything. Well, not quite everything, but the closest to everything anyone knew about the author Charlotte Day.

"I can't be bothered doing my own promo work any more, and this is easier than being dragged around ghastly book signings or speaking at terrible author events."

"I agree, you'll do yourself a disservice by going to events if you feel negatively about them, but not this."

Michael and I never argued. We talked. We tossed the pros and cons forward and back weighing up the best options. Usually we agreed, but not now.

"Much as I hate them," he said, "I think you should consider putting your books up as ebooks instead of this ... ghastly whatever-it-is publicity deal."

"One day maybe I will, but I don't like them either. I like real books, and I believe my target audience and age group do too. My readers aren't going to use technology to find me anyway. I just need someone to keep talking about me, so my name is always around for the media to pick up. Ray is perfect for that. He is guaranteed to boast about his clients."

"So what's going on with this girl?"

"Not sure," I admitted. "I don't know what she expects from all these interviews. I can't make up my mind whether it's a series in a literary magazine or a book deal. The latter, I think. But I'm enjoying the attention ... and the opportunity to recall much of my life. Surely any publicity is good?" I was playing devil's advocate and knew it.

"The problem, Charlotte Rose ..." Oh, dear. He used my full name. "How much do you want people to know about you? How much does Ray really know about you?"

I knew exactly what he was saying. I wrote under different names. Only Michael and Luke knew them all, and thanks to Luke, I published my 'other' books in secret. Michael was as worried as I as to what I would give away during these interviews that Emma could use to my disadvantage. He'd be even more perturbed at the risks involved if he knew about the other me, the one before Charlotte.

"I'll be as careful now as I've always been, Michael." I always called him by his full name. He didn't suit being a Mike.

"Does he come round here often?"

"Who?"

"Ray, of course." He sounded exasperated with me.

"No. I don't like him coming round. He's out of place here and annoys me. I deal with him mostly by email or phone. Why?"

Michael shrugged. "I worry about you."

He'd avoided my question, but I let it lie. We changed the subject and chatted about my roses as we took a stroll around the garden. I loved them with a passion, feeding and nurturing them with great care.

The rose formed my brand. I used it as the logo on all my books, employing different styles and shapes depending on the genre.

To me, the rose symbolises life. From a small, tight bud, like a newborn baby wrapped in a cocoon, before emerging into a perfect bloom, with its upright outer petals and deep heart, just like an adolescent. Then the sunshine spreads the petals further, just as we humans learn about life, absorbing both love and hate. Finally the rose lies open and spent, exhausted by the seasons' trauma of wind and rain, to slowly drop its petals and fade away, as do we who become old and invisible.

"Who are you being today?" he asked suddenly.

Keeping my head down, I reached out to inhale the perfume from a perfect rose and avoided his gaze. "Just me, Michael. I'm always just me. You know that. I'm not psychotic or delusional."

"Your voices are quite distinct when you write, but I can't always tell in person. You hide."

I could tell he was still trying to attract my eye. I reached further away for another adolescent rose – hiding, exactly as he said I did.

"I only write as Georgina when the darkest moods are on me."

"Why Georgina?

"Because Georgie knows me and can say things I can't."

"So who is Amanda Grove?"

"Amanda is who I always wanted to be – a free spirit. Why all these questions? You know all this. You've always known."

Again, he avoided my question, staring at me as I turned to face him, studying me, reaching deep into my mind trying to find the real me. In the end, he took my face between his hands, kissed me on the forehead and simply said, "Be careful."

Emma

I'm not sure what's changed, but she's told me to call her Charlotte, and she's letting me visit twice a week. It's like she's accepted the idea of a ghostwritten biography and is surprisingly keen to get on with her story. I often get to stay longer than the designated hour before she sends me on my way again.

But her reticence – no, that's not quite the right word, her furtiveness – has increased. She is hiding something. I'm certain of it. She still won't let me record anything. She's telling me stories at length, sometimes very funny ones, embellishing with word pictures one minute then changing the subject the next. Other times, she'll stop a story partway through, skipping over years and places, and no amount of prompting gets me closer to those missing sections.

I am so frustrated. All my Internet searches have come up blank. I didn't find anything new, and Ray knows nothing, despite him boasting about how well he's figured her out. His bluff and bravado are starting to get on my nerves. I'd love to tell him where to go, but if I did, I would lose my access to Charlotte.

I'll just have to put up with him for a while longer. I'm surprised she is putting up with him at all.

She's a wily old bird. She had me laughing at some of her anecdotes, and I found myself telling her one or two stories of my own, but I don't want to go down that track.

I mustn't let myself like her too much or I'll never get this project finished. How I'm going to fill in the gaps and get her to let me in on those so obvious secrets I have no idea.

Neither have I had an opening to ask about the photograph. I must have seen it before somewhere. But where? I need to ask her about it.

Charlotte

End of March

I hate doctors. I don't know why I bother to go, they can't fix what's wrong. They are such harbingers of doom, always prodding and poking around and full of questions and instructions:

"Do you eat a balanced diet?" ... "Yes, I do."

"Do you smoke?" ... "Not any more."

"Do you drink?" ... "Yes, I enjoy a glass or two of wine. Everything in moderation," I smiled, (*except when I'm miserable, then I drink a lot*).

"You do know it's terminal, don't you?" ... "Yes, I do. I've suspected so for some time. I can read." (*Do you really have to confirm it?*)

"You shouldn't self-diagnose, you know." ... "Yes, I know, but it's too late to change."

I got away from her as quickly as possible, saying I would think about her advice to ease the pain when it got bad and what treatment I should undertake. Fat chance. At home, I poured a large glass of red wine, wrapped a blanket around my knees and sat in my snug.

I understand why Michael was so adamant I be careful. Emma is worming her way into my life and my thoughts when she is not here, forcing me to remember things I thought I'd forgotten. I'm even allowing her more time than I first stipulated. She will take advantage if I let her, I know, but she is mellowing too, just a little. She softens when she laughs. I'm glad I've been able to make her laugh. I suspect she hasn't had much of it in her life. The few snippets she's told me about herself, all of which I added to my notebook about her, tells me she is hiding a lot too. It takes one to know one, so the saying goes. We are both playing the hedging game.

How much am I prepared to remember? Do I care any more what people think? My shame, my feelings of inadequacy and my inability to be myself have led me to where I am today, hiding behind pseudonyms and avoiding the truth. Who am I, really?

Am I the Rose-Anne Thomas I was born; the Charlotte Rose Day I became; my alter ego Amanda Grove who writes about the love and romance I never had; or my best friend Georgina Strong who writes of injustice? It doesn't matter. We'll all be gone soon.

I feel myself slipping into the real world of my past more often than I care to since Emma has appeared on the scene. Not that she would ever learn about the time Georgie, my lifelong imaginary friend, first appeared in my life.

I was six.

*****

Our new life on the southern coast settled into a routine. My mother ran a bed and breakfast which, during the war, had mostly been for refugees, but as they returned to their homes afterwards, a small visitor trade started up again. My mother was extra busy with the cooking and cleaning; my father charmed the guests when he served at table. In between meal times, he took the large delivery tricycle with its cart between the front wheels into town to sell cigarettes and stockings, or crisps and chocolate, or whatever luxuries he could get his hands on. He was the sort of charmer who could sell his soul to the devil and come out clean. I remember him saying the Yanks were useful to trade with.

When my parents were busy, I was sent to play.

All the boxes of supplies were stored in the shed at the top of the steps behind the house. In those days, the little bags of salted potato crisps came in large tins – dozens and dozens to each tin. I was strictly forbidden to open the tins, which were all sealed around the top edge anyway, but sometimes if a tin was already open I would sneak a packet when I was hungry, being careful to hide the wrapping.

I would use the empty tins to decorate my little hidey-hole – one for a seat, stacking others up to make a dressing table – then pick the ones with the shiniest sides to polish up as a mirror. The image was distorted but it didn't matter. I would pretend to be a princess or a movie star or a singer. I loved singing. I played doctors and nurses. I dressed my dolls and talked to my imaginary friends. I learnt to keep out of sight.

Sometimes my father would come in and catch me there. I remembered how my throat tightened and my heart thumped.

"Ah. There you are. Have you been eating the crisps again?"

"No, Father." I backed up against the wall as far away as I could.

"I don't believe you. You must be punished for lying to me." He sat down on two tins. "Take your underpants off, come here and bend over my knee."

I bit my lip and shook my head, but he had a hard, glittery look in his eyes that frightened me.

"Now." His voice was icy.

I did as I was told. He lifted my skirt and placed his hand squarely on my backside. Sometime he would smack me slowly and hard, one stroke at a time, taking care to land each hand carefully in time with a grunt. Other times he would tap me fast and furiously, moaning as he did so until there was a final whack, and he would sigh deeply. I would try not to cry or call out, as that would make the smacking longer and faster.

"Get dressed," he ordered. "And never lie to me again, and don't you go telling tales to anyone or you'll get another dose."

I nodded and hurriedly pulled on my knickers, knowing as I did that there would always be another time. That's when Georgie came into my life. I could tell her everything, and she would listen without passing judgment.

Summer passed, and the guests left. The only thing I liked about winter was that I didn't have to share my parents' bedroom any more. I could have the large front room facing the beach all to myself. The room had a double bed and windows that stretched from one wall to the other, facing the view. I loved the two sets of windows, which let me open the inside ones to listen to the howling wind, while the outer set kept the weather out. I could also leave the curtains open and watch the moon and the stars shining way up in the sky.

*****

The phone disturbed my reverie.

"Lottie! How's things, sweetie?" Ray's voice on the other end of the line instantly provoked me to rudeness. I was not his 'sweetie' under any circumstances. And I hated it when he called me Lottie. Rude bastard.

"What do you want?" I really did need to get rid of him. He was no longer any use to me despite his achievements over the last decade.

Nothing fazed Ray. "I just thought I'd see how you were getting on with that journalist girl. What's her name?"

"You should know. You sent her to me."

"Oh, give us a break, sweetie ..."

"Don't call me sweetie! One more comment like that and you're fired."

Goodness, I had let the evil witch out of the cage, I thought, suddenly feeling pleased. Emma's visits had made me face the past I had kept hidden for sixty years, but no more. I would relive my past and think about it coherently from the distance of time and decide whether to keep it hidden or share it. I didn't have the answer right now but making the decision to revisit everything lifted a huge weight from my shoulders.

Ray suddenly became much more circumspect and polite, apologising for upsetting me and telling me what he had planned in the way of exposure and promotion.

"Just leave it for now, will you please, Ray? I'm not satisfied with my latest efforts, and I've put them in the drawer until I can give them further consideration."

By the time he'd finished blustering about keeping my name in the public eye and not losing momentum, I'd had enough. "Stop. I don't need you, and I don't need promotion any more – I have more than enough titles out there. I'm terminating our contract. I'll ring you if and when I want to use your services again."

I hung up.

He'd be furious and try to ignore the fact I'd just fired him. He would worry about what would happen to the story Emma was supposed to be writing and what impact it would have on him, but I had no intention of letting him know I proposed carrying on with Emma. I wanted to know her story. I wanted to tell *my* story. I wanted someone to know the truth. I wouldn't worry Michael.

The next time she came, I would have another story for her ... but some fragments could not be shared, not ever. There were some things I would never, could never, speak about. They were almost too hard for me to remember.

*****

He came to my room – my special wintertime room. The one I treasured because it was mine. I didn't have to share any more. He came to punish me again, but this night my mother discovered him there.

"Don't you dare touch her," she screamed, flaying at him. "Get out, you filthy dog. Get out!"

I hid under the bedclothes as her voice reached fever pitch.

"I swear I'll kill you. If you so much as touch her again, I will kill you."

Peeking over the top of the blankets, I couldn't see my mother's face. Her back was to me. His face was a deep red, like he was boiling and ready to explode. I'd never seen a look like that on anyone's face before. I had no words to describe it but it frightened me.

He never touched me again, but I soon learnt that when I made him angry he would punish my mother instead. I was ten.

I closed my eyes. I still had five more years to block out before the new me began.

Emma

Well! Who would have guessed? Pseudonyms! What a surprise. Not that I let on. No way was I letting her know I found it startling, or even slightly more interesting than anything else I had garnered about her. But how has she kept them secret for so long?

I will need to find out more about these names she's used and see where they lead, but I suspect nowhere. Charlotte wouldn't have kept them hidden this long and then revealed them if she thought there was dirt to find. No, this was her way of telling me how skilful she is as a writer: changing genres and voice and being successful at all three. She said we'd talk more about her novels next time I visited. But I bet it's a promo stunt to advance all her books. Cunning witch, it's such a good ploy to reveal material like this in a biography. I bet Ray put her up to it. That would be something he would do. I'm really getting to dislike that man intensely.

She's pumping me more and more about my reactions to her stories, asking if there are any comparisons with my life, or something similar I've written about. Some days I admit there are and will let through a small scrap. But I need to be careful. She will do her own research one day and check up on me. I don't think it's occurred to her yet she might be able to find information about me on the Net. But then, two of us can play at hiding behind names.

I've sensed an underlying outrage sometimes in the way she speaks, but it's waning. She's sounding more disillusioned and detached, tired even. Some stories are still full of enthusiasm: she enjoys showing me items from her china cabinet and telling me their individual story. Not all are her mother's or grandmother's; many were gifts to her. She remembers exactly where she got them, or who gave them to her – mostly mementoes from the stage, or maybe secret admirers. Michael, maybe? She talks about him a lot. Others? I'm sure she only tells me part of the story. These are the times when she sounds disconnected.

Some bits rang bells in my life, not that I'm letting on to that either. She feels the loss of her mother greatly, but I'm not sure why. I can't even find out when her mother died, or how, come to think of it. That might be significant. Maybe she was quite young when it happened. Does Charlotte blame herself? She keeps repeating how safe she felt in her mother's love.

Unlike Charlotte, I just feel anger when I think of my mother. She let me down, and I will never forgive her. I don't think I'll ever feel safe again.

Charlotte

April

I'd left the front door open. "Come on in," I called from the kitchen when I heard Emma's knock. "Would you like to stay for lunch?"

Closing the door behind her, she entered the kitchen. "That would be lovely," she answered graciously with only a flicker of surprise crossing her face.

We had reached the first name stage but, needing to conserve my energy, I'd been strict about keeping to an appointed time, only sometimes allowing myself a little leeway. I'm sure she noticed.

"I just thought if you wanted to talk about my time on the stage at any length or get more in depth about my books it might take a bit longer."

"Good idea."

If I thought Emma would give me any other response, it died at that moment. The mask had come down again as soon as it had lifted. More casually dressed today in smart jeans and a fitting red top and matching low-heeled shoes, she managed to appear stylish whatever she wore. Even so, this was one unhappy young woman, I thought, hiding behind an image of cool disregard. She had a habit of biting the quick at the side of her polished nails, and she constantly gnaws at her bottom lip. She thinks I don't notice.

I threw the quiche together and put it in the oven, wiped my hands on the towel and, pouring the coffee, suggested we sit in my snug by the old coal range. The cooler autumn days were creeping in, and while it's a special time of the year, my aching old bones shiver at the slightest change in temperature.

"Your revelations about your pseudonyms sent me off on a reading spree. I can see why people would never suspect; your topics, genre and voice are quite different. Can you tell me more about why you decided to use pseudonyms?"

Pleased she'd been able to find them all in the library – and had made the effort to at least read the blurb and flick through one or two, enough to understand the difference at any rate – I wondered how to frame my answer. After she'd left last time, I'd questioned my reasoning in telling her and analysing why I suddenly wanted her to know. I'm still not sure I answered myself sufficiently well enough, but the principal motive remained: I didn't want everything I'd written lost after I'd gone, especially Georgie's words.

Emma was an intelligent and informed conversationalist. We talked about social issues, injustices, human rights, wars and values, all the topics Georgie liked to write about. We enjoyed the raillery as we put up supportive arguments and counterarguments, but I began to notice an edge to her voice, and her questions were slightly scornful.

"How can you possibly write about experiences you have no first-hand experience of?"

"Some things you can't write about successfully. I can't dream up the strategic thinking of warfare, or what a surgeon has running through their brain during an operation, even with all the research I do. But when you've lived as long as I have and if you read widely enough, you can write about emotions and reactions. If you have ever had a strong emotional response to anything, or been horrified by an account of man's inhumanity to man, then you can write about it." I watched her face closely.

"But if you've not experienced those emotions how can you understand how someone else feels?" Emma's tone laid bare her scepticism; disbelieving that empathy would serve well enough. "Different people must feel emotion differently, even with similar experiences."

"I understand passion and deeply held feelings, and I simply transform them to suit."

We argued over the concept for quite some time.

"How can you possibly know how I felt when my ..." she paused. Swallowed. "When someone died?"

She'd let down her guard there, I thought.

"I can't. And I don't intend to try. I'm sorry you've lost someone - close?" She ignored the intimation. "But you're missing the point," I coaxed. "You're making this a personal assessment of how I think you feel. I can't. What I can do is instil my characters with what *I* feel. I may not have loved the way you have loved, but my characters can love my way. I can write about love if I've felt something akin."

I could tell Emma didn't believe me. I suspect her training had been clinical, based on fact, not on emotion. She couldn't see how you could transfer emotions. Or else something had left her unable to trust her emotions, and she was deliberately shutting them off.

Her questions had become increasingly antagonistic, but I tried not to rise to the bait. Michael would have been proud of me; Ray wouldn't have believed it possible for me to hold my temper in check.

"So why the three names and three styles if you can transfer feelings?"

I sighed. I was almost surprised at myself. I was being exceptionally patient with this girl. Why? I wondered. I normally wouldn't tolerate that tone of voice from anyone.

"Let's see. Because they are different, maybe?" I knew I was being facetious the minute I opened my mouth and immediately felt mean. "No, sorry. That doesn't answer your question." It was my turn to pause. "Maybe, because if you try to crowd too many ideas into one story it becomes confused. As Charlotte, I write contemporary family novels about the realities and tragedies of life. Amanda writes as a free spirit about love and romance, the feel-good stuff that makes the world comfortable, the wishful things in life. Georgina writes about justice, about righting wrongs. When something happened that I thought outrageous or unfair, I would use her voice to protest. Dissension didn't suit the stories Charlotte wrote about, and only Amanda can write about romantic love."

I looked at her as she flicked her hair behind her ear and bit her lip. She wanted to ask something but didn't.

"I could have written a book in the style of Amanda or Georgina under my own name, but I chose different names and personalities instead. But I bet if you made comparisons about how some of the characters respond to a similar emotion, you would understand what I've been talking about." It was time to break up the conversation. "Lunch?"

I could tell she was getting upset but whatever was eating at her, now was not the right time to broach the subject. I suggested she toss the salad together from the bowls I'd prepared, while I set the table in the dining area. I decided to crack open a bottle of white wine. Either it would loosen her tongue or settle her down.

Over lunch, Emma asked more about Georgie, she being the odd one out of the trio, the one who tackled social issues head on. Somehow, we got onto the subject of whether an adult is a product of their childhood. Whether an individual's response to events and subjects is a reflection of how they were brought up, something inherent they were born with, or created by the societal influence of their peers. She wholeheartedly believed young adults learnt how *not* to be from their parents, not *how* to be.

"I'm who I am because of me and no one else. I do things my way," she said quite forcefully. "The one thing I learnt from my mother was never to believe anyone. I hope I never make her mistakes or treat people the way she did."

The wine certainly hadn't calmed her down. She seemed even more agitated than before. From a greater distance both in age and experience, I couldn't entirely agree.

"But you did learn something. And more than one thing, I think. We never stop learning. We learn from each other, we learn from reading, we learn from our experiences, and yes, we do have inherent traits that mould our responses, but our instinctive emotional responses are a product of consistent modelling when we were young."

Deciding to change the subject to something more light-hearted, I started to talk about Amanda, my romantic idealist who loved love.

"But she's so lightweight and clichéd." Emma dismissed Amanda.

"Is she?" I smiled. At least I'd stirred up a more typical reaction even as I wondered how much of Amanda's stories Emma had actually read, other than the blurb. "Doesn't some small part of us want to believe in perfect love even if we think it's impossible?"

She laughed for the first time since she'd arrived. Maybe the wine was helping after all.

"Maybe I did, once, but I soon found such things belong in fairy tales."

"But you see, I do believe in perfect love."

She looked incredulous. "How can you? How can

you believe in something like that? You don't know how destructive love can be."

I had clearly opened a can of worms, but she changed tack before I could say anything.

"Have you ever been in love?" she asked.

"Of course." I answered without hesitation, except I was kidding myself. I'd never loved the way she meant. I'd been infatuated once in my naïve teenage way. I'd had lovers from time to time but never had a man to love or love me in return and told myself I didn't need one. Only Amanda needed to know about love.

"Tell me about him?"

"I don't think there ever was one 'him'. Love comes in many shapes and sizes. To me love is about feeling safe. To be one's self around people and in places surrounded by the things you love. I love Michael, very much, as I loved Kate, his wife. None of it is, or was, sexual. If you can't find that level of safety then you haven't found perfect love."

Suddenly she was belittling and dismissing quotes like 'make love not war', the anti-war slogan of the sixties and Tennyson's more poetic 'it's better to have loved and lost than never to have loved at all' and denying their essence.

I didn't argue. I sent her off with instructions to read Dorothy Law Nolte's poem from the seventies, 'Children Learn What They Live'.

Emma

Give me strength! What was that sentimental crap about 'perfect love'? What the hell does *she* know about real love? For the life of me, I can't understand why Amanda Grove is as popular as she is. Maybe there are people who want to spend their life in fairyland, but not me, thank you.

The Internet is the most powerful social weapon influencing everything people do these days. She really is yesterday's leftovers with her ideals. I could tell her a thing or two about love and how it always lets you down. Maybe I will one day, just to show her what it's like.

Love does not mean security.

And as for that 'Children Learn What They Live' rubbish – if you believe that you need your head read. I could write my own IF story – starting with IF that bastard hadn't cheated on me; IF my baby, my Ruby, hadn't died; IF my mother hadn't ... (I couldn't even put it into words.) IF my father hadn't run off, then maybe I'd have one person who loved me. IF ... if only! Nothing I learnt from my childhood is worth a damn. I'd have given my life for Ruby: that's the closest I've ever come to a perfect love. Is that what she means? Nah! That's not the love of books.

She's getting under my skin, and I'm letting my guard down too easily. I did not intend to tell her anything about my life, and then I blurt it out like some bolshie teenager. Believe me, Charlotte Day, I know everything there is to know about love – it means nothing but pain and loss.

I'm having trouble figuring this woman out. I fully intended to dislike her but I can't.

Damn and blast her!

Part Two

The missing years

Charlotte

1952 South of England

I came home later than usual from my after-school drama class one fine autumn day, as the last vestiges of warmth were fading and winter hovered just around the corner, to find our house surrounded by police cars and an ambulance. I tried to get past and into the house, but one particularly gruff and mean-spirited police officer stopped me. He told me to stand back and not get in the way. "Please tell me what is happening?" I pleaded.

"Nothing to do with you, girlie. Now, away with you."

"But I live here. I have nowhere else to go."

"Ah. Do you really now. So you're the one." He looked me up and down with disdain. "From what I hear, you're to blame for what happened here as much as your mother."

"No. No. It can't be my fault ... Or hers. Truly, it can't," I mumbled, panic setting in. I could feel my heart beating in my chest, my throat thickened and tears threatened. "I don't understand. What's happening?"

"Sounds to me like you two are a real handful. There's been a domestic, but all is quiet now."

A domestic? What?

"They're taking your mother to hospital to calm her down, that's all. She's hysterical."

Oh, of course, he was using police language. Why didn't he just say my parents had had another fight, which meant my father had beaten her up again? How was it my fault?

"Let me see her," I begged, trying again to push my way through.

The policeman pulled me back. He called out, and a policewoman took me into the garden, talking all the while. I hardly heard her. Her words sounded meaningless until she said, "Your mother will be taken to the psychiatric ward at the hospital. You are not allowed in there. You are not old enough. You have to stay with your father."

My heart jolted. I felt sure it stopped then started again, twice as loud, twice as fast. I couldn't stay alone in the house with my father! "No!" I cried. "No! I can't stay with him. I just can't. Please don't make me."

She stared at me with concerned eyes. "Why ever not?"

I hung my head in shame. "You've seen what he does." I couldn't tell her anything else. Tears streamed down my face, and I started to shake uncontrollably.

"Stay here. And don't move until I come back."

I nodded and sat on the garden wall. Minutes passed. Suddenly she and another policewoman reappeared by my side and told me I could stay with a neighbour for the night.

They led me two doors along the street to Mrs Baker's place. She greeted me well enough, murmuring about 'the poor child' and showed me where I could sleep, but I felt uncomfortable. I didn't like the floral wrap-around aprons she wore, and she smelt funny, nothing like my mother's perfumes, and wore a headscarf tied on top of her head. I never understood why she and my mother had become friends; they were so different. But I was cold and couldn't stop shivering, I was glad to be inside.

She ran a hot bath. "Take as long as you like, lovey. I'll just wash your blouse for the morning."

I lay in the bath trying to sort out what had happened and, more importantly, what would happen next, but failed to see the future. I had no idea. Two things I knew: I was scared, and I was alone.

At the dinner table later that night, I tried again to find out what had happened.

"Don't you worry your little head about it," said Mrs Baker. "It will all work out all right in the end. Your mother's in the right place, and when she's calmed down she'll be home again right as rain before you know it."

I didn't believe her. Something told me this was serious, it was not like the normal beatings my mother had taken before. I knew my life was about to change, but why was everyone being so secretive? I talked to my imaginary friend Georgie about it endlessly.

She didn't try to pretend all was well or ask dumb questions. She just listened without saying anything or telling me to stop acting like a brat.

I could not sleep. I lay in the bed in my borrowed nightie, restless and fearful. I even piled my school cardy and blazer on top of the one blanket covering my bed to try and warm myself up and stop the shaking, but failed. I tossed and turned remembering all sorts of incidents: the time my mother had put some sort of laxative powder in my father's dinner to give him gut ache after another beating, and the time my father turned up to my school musical.

I remember the feeling of horror as he came storming down the hall, shouting. The actors stopped speaking, the audience stared, a teacher tried to block his way, but nothing stopped him. "Get down here, you. Now!" he demanded. "You are coming home with me. I did not give you permission to be out of the house."

I walked through the wings, down the stairs and met him in front of the stage, still in full costume.

He dragged me by the arm through the school hall while everyone in the audience turned to gaze after me, whispering. I was so embarrassed.

"I'll sort your mother out later."

And he did. Like he always did.

There were other times like that. Times when I sat beside my mother's hospital bed as she recovered from yet another so-called stomach upset or bowel stoppage. He was careful not to hit her so hard he broke a bone, but he would punch her in the stomach or in the back. The bruises changed from black to yellow before he would hit her again. Over time, she had a series of what they called nervous breakdowns. They would give her electric shock treatment and drug her so much that she slurred her words and slept more often than she was awake – until she came home again. My mother stopped lying to me when I turned twelve and let me see my father as he really was. I couldn't understand then, or since, why he was so popular with other people. How he could charm other people into believing he was the rational and reasonable husband and father, and my mother the hysterical, unreasonable woman who fell down stairs or walked into doors and self-harmed. How did he do that?

Somehow I got to school the next day, I don't remember that part. I remember being called into the headmistress's office.

"Sit down, Rose-Anne," she said kindly. The grim look on her face had frightened me. "I'm sorry it has to be me who breaks the news." She paused for quite some time, seemingly searching for the right words. "I have been informed by the police that your mother died overnight. I am so sorry."

I sat staring at her, unable to comprehend what she had just said. What did she mean my mother was dead? How? Why? She couldn't be, could she? She was all right yesterday. They said so. They said she was hysterical. How can anybody hysterical be dead?

"I've been told to keep you at school until someone from welfare comes to talk to you and explain what will happen next."

Welfare? I didn't understand. Why welfare?

"Rose-Anne. I'm sorry you'll have to wait for the welfare people. They will find you a place to live for the next few months until you turn fifteen. In the meantime, I suggest you return to class to take your mind off it."

I did as I was told. I had always done as I was told. Everyone stared at me when I returned to take my seat. My classmate Beth handed me a hanky whispering sorry under her breath. Everyone knew; lessons continued. I was expected to carry on as if nothing had changed.

How does that happen? How does life go on even when something so momentous strikes that you feel the world spinning around in a hazy swirl of fog and noise as you stand dead still in the middle trying to catch on to something solid.

The welfare lady came and took me to a place to stay with a House Mother and House Father and five other girls like me. She introduced everyone and showed me around, her voice upbeat and false, trying to create excitement in the changes to my life.

"Why am I here?" I asked once we were alone in the room that was to be mine. Except it wouldn't be all mine. I had to share. I'd never shared before.

"I thought you had been told, dear. Your mother has died," she said.

"Yes. I know that. But why am I here? I want to see my mother."

"Oh, no, Rose-Anne. That's not possible. We can't allow that." The woman pursed her lips, and a deep frown creased her brow.

"Why not? Why can't I see her?"

"Sit down, Rose." She pointed to the bed and pulled up the solitary chair. "I'm not sure why you haven't been told this, but since you will soon be able to choose the path your life will take, I suppose you should know."

This sounded even more serious than I had imagined. And she had called me Rose. No one called me Rose. My mother insisted on my full name.

Fidgeting uncomfortably on the chair, the woman continued. "Your mother's death is now a police investigation. There will be an inquest into her death, and charges are being laid against your father."

Charges? I wondered whether someone had finally believed my mother.

"Manslaughter, I believe. Possibly murder."

When I didn't respond the welfare lady continued. "Didn't anyone tell you? Your mother died as a result of the injuries she received during the domestic altercation."

Why did everyone use such big words? What she meant was my father had finally killed my mother. I was not surprised.

"Since your father is your next of kin and therefore your legal guardian, you have been made a ward of the state until your fifteenth birthday in February. Until then, the state decides where you will live. Once you turn fifteen you can choose. Be patient, finish your schooling and take your leaving exams next month."

She stood, put the chair back in the corner by the window, gathered up her folders lying on the desk and opened the door.

"Be good. I'll be back in a week to check on you."

Somehow I survived the next few months, went to school and scraped through my exams. I withdrew from my friends, only talking to the house parents or the welfare people when I had to. It all passed in a blur.

While the whole country, all gloomy and sad, mourned the loss of their beloved King George VI, I learnt about grief and loss. But they could soften their grief by celebrating the history-making coronation of Queen Elizabeth II. I couldn't see such a glorious future for me.

Christmas came and went, and even though the house parents made an effort, it wasn't like I remembered, or wanted. We were each given a small gift – a handkerchief, socks, lipstick or some such thing. I hated it. I stayed silent all day, escaping to my room as soon as I could. I lay on my bed staring at the ceiling.

I had been allowed to attend my mother's funeral accompanied by the house parents, but it had been a strange experience. Hardly anyone had been there, not even my father, and the man taking the service obviously hadn't known her. All the things he said about her bore no resemblance to the person I knew. I vaguely wondered who had told him what to say, but it didn't matter, I knew her story.

*****

My fifteenth birthday arrived and a small group gathered at the house to wish me well and say goodbye. The welfare lady gave me some legal papers, advice pamphlets and a bankbook in a neat brown file. In a semi-trance, it all passed me by. With so many decisions to make as to what to do with my life, I hardly knew where to start.

The date of my father's trial had been set. I'd been called as a witness but I sat in the vast chamber, too terrified to speak, with my teeth chattering and tears rolling down my face. Finally, I answered their questions in a small side room and was allowed to go.

The lawyer handling everything told me I had inherited my mother's personal effects, her jewellery and her china cabinet. I could take what I wanted now and collect the cabinet from storage when I was ready. Whatever happened to the rest of the furniture or the house, I never knew or even thought about. They said I had enough money to set myself up and would receive small, regular payments until the bulk of the money came through when I turned twenty-one.

"Don't worry your little head about it, dear. Someone will handle it all for you. They'll take care of you."

But I still needed to find somewhere to live and earn my own money. Unable to cope with the thought of living and working in the town where it all happened, I moved to Bristol, to be an unknown in a city of many. Deciding what sort of a job I wanted turned into a bigger challenge than I'd expected, so I turned to my one passion in life – musical theatre.

I joined a choir, auditioned for and won a part with the local musical theatre group, signed up with a talent agency and went to work in a jewellery factory assembling chains with rings and clasps. I lived in a boarding house, changed my clothes, my hair and adopted a stage name. I became Charlotte Rose Day, performer – Lottie to my friends.

My life became a whirlwind. In the rock and roll era, no one questioned why someone so young should be alone. Freedom was on everyone's lips. I rushed from the factory to choir practice and show rehearsals and worked hard, trying to be better than everyone else, to be important, to be valued, to be the best. When I sang, I was transformed into someone else entirely. My voice soared with the ebb and flow of the music, with the drama and emotion. When on stage, I became the character demanded by the script. I danced with the best of them, watching and learning quickly, and mastered the knack of pretending to be someone other than me.

Winter turned to summer, and the moments of unexpected grief were getting easier. I could listen to my mother's voice in my head – usually serving a warning about my behaviour – without crying every time. I turned to my faithful Georgie at these times and we talked – or rather, I talked and she listened – until I could talk no more. I was still a child in many ways, with all the insecurities and gaucheness of a teenager trying to be grown up and not always succeeding, but I never let anyone see my fear. I kept to myself, not saying much, watching and observing, learning about this new world I had entered.

At work, I sat at my table monotonously linking rings to chains and passing them on to the next person. I listened to the gossip around me but didn't get involved, waiting for the day to end so I could escape into my world of make-believe.

Opening night! The long months of rehearsal for *Carousel* finally ended, and I buzzed with excitement, barely able to keep still, and broke one of theatre's biggest rules. I peeked through the side curtains to watch the audience settling into their seats, waiting in anticipation.

"Get away from there, girl," whispered the stage manager, making me jump.

"Sorry. I'm new to all this and just wanted to see."

"Don't care about any of that. You don't look through the curtains on my watch. Be off."

Chastened, I retreated to the corridor. The local church hall proved barely adequate for the performance. The cast sang and danced their hearts out, trying in their minds to raise the somewhat seedy surroundings to that of the big London theatres. The crew made sure the lights were on at the right time, the set moved seamlessly and the show ran like clockwork. The audience was not disappointed; their spontaneous applause was our reward. We ran off the stage to our makeshift quarters at the back of the hall with energy I'd never known before.

Dressing rooms are always cramped, chaotic places with girls in various states of undress, cosmetics and tissues strewn all over the dressing tables, the lights harsh on tired faces, but alive like no other place I had ever been. I loved every minute of every show and moved from one to the next without a break.

A year passed. I'm not sure how I would have coped without Georgie, my dearest, truest, if imaginary, friend. I learnt a lot about life from watching others, from listening. I got better and more skilled and rose above the chorus line to a small part with a few words, or a solo dance routine, but inside I still felt insecure. I trusted no one, told no one my story.

At the beginning of the following year, I changed troupes and won a leading role. Deciding I should celebrate, I drummed up enough courage to ask some of the girls to join me for supper after rehearsal. We went to the milk bar and played the jukebox, and ate fish and chips from the newspaper as we walked home. I felt happier than I'd been in a long while. Georgie didn't come with me; she didn't mix well with strangers.

Opening night of the spring show was another great success, and as usual, the girls all noisily careered down the corridor to the changing rooms.

Partway along the corridor, Tom, the director stopped me, putting his arm around my shoulder. "That was excellent, Lottie. I am most impressed. I'm sorry we haven't had this conversation before. I should have asked. Where did you learn your skills?"

"At school and some classes. I loved doing drama and dance, but I've learnt a lot more doing real shows since," I replied innocently.

"Really? Is that all? You've never had professional coaching?"

"No. Sir."

"It's Tom. We don't stand on ceremony around here." He turned me around to face him and placed a hand on each shoulder, lowering his head slightly, capturing me in his hold and anchoring me with his eyes. "I think you could really go places, Lottie. I have some ideas. I think I can help you." His face moved closer to mine, and I instinctively pulled my head back. Whatever he intended to say, he changed his mind, dropping his hands from my shoulders. "Let me make a few phone calls." With a quick kiss on my cheek, he was gone.

I ran into the dressing room to get changed. Some of the girls still sat at the mirrors, wiping away the heavy stage make-up with thick cold cream.

As she looked up into the mirror, Maggie, one of the older girls who'd been with the troupe for quite a while, spotted me coming in. "Ooo. Look at you," she said. "Chatting it up with the maestro. Watch yourself, girl. He'll have you on the director's couch before you know what hit you." She carried on wiping her face, watching me out of the corner of her eye.

"Director's couch? What's that?"

The girls all laughed.

"Don't play the innocent with me," said Maggie.

Seeing the confused look on my face, she got up from her chair and stood in front of me, suddenly solicitous. "If you really don't know, then be careful is all I can say. He's got quite a reputation has our Tom."

Whatever Tom's reputation might have been, he was kind to me. I'll never know how he did it, but he set me up with Rodney, a professional coach who had been with the Bristol Old Vic Theatre School. Between these lessons and the three nights of rehearsals for the next show, my evenings were now so busy my landlady complained I was never there.

"By golly, girl. You'll wear yourself out with all this gallivanting," she said as she put my dinner on the table.

"Oh, I'll be fine, Mrs Sweet," I answered, shovelling the food into my mouth as fast as I could.

"Slow down, girl. Appreciate the food you have. You'll get a tummy ache if you're not careful."

"Sorry. It's just I'll be late otherwise. I really appreciate you cooking for me like this. It's special." I grinned apologetically with my mouth full, making me feel like a gargoyle with huge puffy cheeks.

"Get away with you. Don't you go getting sentimental on me now? I'm just doing what you pays me for."

"No. You do more than that. You know you do, and I thank you." I stood and gave her a quick hug before racing out the door.

"Poor wee lass. Alone in the world she is." I heard her say to a fellow boarder entering as I skipped down the front steps. "And so young."

As I strode down the street, I hugged the thought to me that someone cared. Tom cared for me too.

The months passed and my coach Rodney put me through some exhausting routines: stretching my vocal chords, learning to fill my lungs with air and slowly letting it out again for longer notes, learning vibrato sounds to make my lips loose to enunciate better. Three hours a week – one singing, one dancing and one acting. Every muscle in my body was stretched into angles I didn't think possible. I was made to walk, turn, sit, frown, smile, glare and use my body to create language and expression, all without saying a word, until I was exhausted.

But Rodney was a delightful character. I adored him right from the start. He was old – well, old to my tender years – skinny and funny. He dressed in tight trousers, with shiny soft leather shoes, an open-necked shirt with a cravat, and a flamboyant waistcoat, donning an incongruous tweed jacket and beret when he went out. He told me he had once been a dance star until he broke his leg in a freak fall. It never healed properly, so instead he became a teacher.

Tom was my constant shadow during this time. He would meet me after my sessions with Rodney and take me for a cup of tea and a sandwich before rehearsals or the show. After, he was always the last to leave and often invited me to stay behind and talk.

"Let's put some of what Rodney has taught you into practice." He led me onto the stage and flicked on the working lights.

"Show me what a girl in love would do to let her man know she loved him."

He demanded more expression, more intuition and more interpretation.

Time passed. I began to forget the shivering sense of fear that had grown whenever my father came near. With Tom, it was a shiver of excitement, a vibrancy I'd never felt before. I became someone else on the stage and in his arms.

"Here. Let me show you." He'd kiss me deeply, his hands moving slowly over my body, which responded to his touch with a desperate passion. He was steadfast, plausible and persuasive, and his patience was finally rewarded. Nothing I'd experienced so far had prepared me for the explosion of feelings Tom aroused in me. I hugged them to me. I was in love: a secret I kept between me and Georgie.

For two years, I starred in shows: *Salad Days* was my first, then *Chu Chin Chow, South Pacific, Oklahoma, The King and I* and others. My big break, thanks to Rodney – and Tom, of course – came with *The Boyfriend.* Tom stuck by me every step of the way. As my star rose, I was showered with gifts, flowers, invites to parties and received more than my share of passes from young men, older men, men who wanted more than I had to give. I didn't want them. I had Tom. But I misread these feelings, reading more into them than was there and misunderstood his intentions. As soon as I stopped being useful to him, he dropped me, and without his patronage my star faded as fast as it had risen.

The third anniversary of my mother's passing came round. I expected it, of course, but never thought I'd feel the way I did this time. I woke that morning with a deep sense of foreboding as if something heavy sat on my chest. I could hardly breathe. I got up quickly, ran to the bathroom and was violently ill. I washed and dressed as fast as I could, my sense of panic rising all the time. I rushed down the stairs to the kitchen hoping to find Mrs Sweet.

"Good morning, dear," she said brightly, as she stirred the large pot of porridge on the stove without turning around.

I raced over. Impulsively, I gave her a hug, surprising her so much she dropped the spoon.

She turned and looked at me. "Oh, you gave me a start! Oh dear. What ever is the matter? You look like you've seen a ghost."

If I hadn't felt so bad, I might have laughed at the

irony in her statement. She thought I was an orphan, but nothing more. No details. I could only shake my head. "Oh. Do I? It's nothing. I'm okay." I dismissed her comments, trying to appear as normal as I could despite the fact my heart was beating loudly in my chest.

"I meant to tell you, dear. There's a registered letter sitting on the dresser over there. Came for you yesterday. Sorry, I didn't give it to you last night, but I was feeling so weary and went to bed 'fore you came in. You were very late." Her tone was slightly reproving.

I walked over to the dresser to retrieve it and recognised the lawyer's name on the envelope. I opened it to find another registered letter inside from Her Majesty's Prison Service and immediately dropped it, frightened of what it might tell me. I stood staring at the envelope, hardly seeing the crossed red lines, the official stamp or my real name written in flowing letters, through the haze of uncertainty. Finally, I picked it up and, getting a knife from the drawer, slit it open. I read the few lines on the pure white page, all in legal talk. I read it again before I completely understood what it said.

The strange feeling I'd had all morning suddenly worsened. A rushing, roaring sound raged inside my head, and everything around me seemed distant, as if I wasn't part of it but somewhere else looking in. I felt rather than saw Mrs Sweet put the pot to one side and move towards me to catch me just as I started to fall. She put her arm around my shoulders and led me to a chair at the table.

"My goodness. You've gone even paler, if that was possible. What is it? What's upset you so much? Come and sit down here, lovey. I'll make you a nice cup of tea. That always helps me when I'm feeling poorly."

Out of the corner of my eye, I could see her studying me as she made the tea. I could hear her voice in the background but not what she was saying.

She had picked the letter up off the floor where I had dropped it.

"Oh, my goodness. Oh, my! Oh, my dear. Who's this man then, who were found guilty of murder? It says 'ere the sentence has been carried out. And what was 'is is now yours. Oh, you poor girl. What 'ardships 'ave you 'ad in your life? Poor lovey, tell me all about it."

Sometime later, I blindly walked down the street, unsure where I was heading but knowing I needed to think. I crossed the road and found a seat in the small park that offered respite to the city dwellers on a hot summer's day. In autumn, it was cool under the trees. I shivered – not only from the cold.

I fumbled in my handbag, grabbing desperately for the pack of cigarettes and my mother's lighter. My hands shook as I extracted one from the packet and put it in my mouth. I flicked the silver lighter case open, holding the flame in cupped hands until finally managing to light the stick of calm and inhaling deeply. Replacing them neatly in my bag, I clicked it shut and leaned back, trying to relax. I rarely smoked, it was bad for my throat, but when I was upset I turned to the vice my mother had favoured. I could hear my father's voice in my head calling out names,

names he used for my mother, for me – tart, slut, whore – and worse.

Georgie appeared at my side. I smiled gratefully. "I'm so scared, Georgie. I wish I was anybody and anywhere else but me, here and now."

A cloud of shame settled deeper over my shoulders. My mother murdered, my father hanged – and I was to blame. At least that's what the policeman said. He said it was my fault. Those words had echoed in my head often since that day it all happened. Whether it was or not didn't matter. I blamed myself either way. "I'm sure everyone knows of my disgrace, my guilt whenever they look at me and I just want to hide."

In the back of my mind, I could hear Georgie trying to persuade me it couldn't be my fault, but her words didn't penetrate.

For a long time I sat in silence, just thinking about what I should do, where my life would lead me and what I wanted to do next.

"I don't know what to feel. I never wanted to see him again ... but this ... This is ..." I didn't have the words.

I was different to other girls. I was ...

That was my problem. I didn't know who I was or what I was. But now I had another problem.

Mrs Sweet was the only person to know my true history, and I left her and it behind as fast as I could – taking more with me than I expected.

Part Three

The here and now

Charlotte

Late April

I have few needs and even fewer wants. I'm happy with my life.

I need my daily walk along the beach, to rejuvenate, but it's getting harder; I get what I need, which isn't much, from the village – I hate the large supermarkets. I'm eating less, but red wine keeps my corpuscles alive. At least that is what I choose to believe. I need time alone, but I want to spend time with my best friend before we are separated for good.

"Happy Birthday, Michael," I'd said when I called earlier.

Our weekly phone conversations have become an essential part of life for both of us. Without them over our latter years, I think both of us would have wandered off into some sort of bleak world inhabited only by one's demons and memories. We keep each other sane in an increasingly self-centred world.

"How are you? Better? ... Good ... Yes, me too. Your Linda tells me the family is getting together this afternoon ..." I'd said. "... Oh, stop fussing. You'd be hurt if they didn't bother, so behave and act your charming self ..." I'd countered, disturbed by his attitude. "Yes. Of course I'll be there. See you later."

Michael worried me; he looked very sallow and ventured out even less than I did. Since his unannounced visit a couple of months ago, he'd not been back. I'd been the one doing the visiting – something very out of the ordinary – but he'd caught a cold and not been able to shake the cough.

I arrived at Michael's around four o'clock to find his daughter Linda, her husband Bob, and their son Matt already there. Matt was Michael's eldest grandchild, but Jessica, Matt's sister, was his favourite. Not that he would admit it, but she reminded him of Kate: similar colouring and a certain turn of her head.

"Hello there," said Linda. "Come in. It's nice to see you again." She kissed my cheek and accepted the bottle of wine. "Are you keeping well? Jessica and her lot are away for the school holidays. Dave and Sharon will be here soon, so will Luke. You know Dave's Ashley is still overseas, don't you? And Chelsea is tied up with something at uni and can't make it." I suppressed a smile at Linda's need to explain. It didn't matter to me which of her brood was there. I'd come to see Michael and Luke.

When I first met Michael, they only had Linda and Dave. A second son came along later, but their late surprise, Luke, was my favourite. At thirty-seven, he'd so far remained a determined single. He reminded me most of Michael at a younger age, but

Linda treated him very much like the baby of the family who had yet to grow up and overruled him in everything.

You don't notice the years rolling by when you are living your own life, doing your own thing, hardly heeding that you've slowed down a bit, but when children have children, who have children, it all gets far too complicated and depressing. Except, of course, Michael didn't find it depressing. He was in his element. He patently loved his grandchildren and great-grandchildren. He'd adopted a winning formula: talking to them about the things that interested them, even if he didn't have a clue about the computer games and jargon they used.

I'm the one who found it all so depressing. I didn't have the necessary relationship skills. I'd never learnt them. I had always been an introvert, and nothing had tempted me to change, which made gatherings like this a trial. If Michael and I hadn't gone back such a long way, I wouldn't have accepted the invitation – except for Luke. He had taken over where Michael had left off and was successfully adapting to the swift changes in the book industry. He was my secret agent.

"Aunt Lottie," said Matt. "Good to see you. Haven't caught up in ages." He hugged me gently and, with hands still on my upper arms, looked at me closely. He frowned. "Are you well?"

What was it with people and my health all of sudden? He didn't wait for my response. "Allison and the kids won't make it today. The little one is sick, so I'll slink off after I've had a chat with the old man."

Michael's children had always called me 'aunt' – except for Luke. He simply called me Charli. I much preferred it. Aunt had been the only acceptable form of address for a family friend back in the sixties and seventies, and his grandchildren had been taught to carry it on. Although I never thought I deserved the title. An aunt should be involved and interested. I never was, apart from Luke. Still anything was better than being called Miss Day.

"Can I help with anything, Linda?" I offered.

"No, thanks. I've got it all under control. There's not so many of us today. I'll organise a big bash for Dad's 80th next year. You just take these and go talk to Dad." Linda handed me two glasses of red wine. "Bob, can you get the door? I hear a car arriving."

I found Michael sitting in the lounge talking with Matt.

"Thanks for the advice, Grandad. It might work." Matt stood up and shook hands with his grandfather. "I'd better be going. Catch up next week."

"What was that all about?" I asked, taking Matt's vacated chair while Michael struggled with another coughing spasm.

He wiped the spittle away with a handkerchief, which he shoved back into his pocket. As the blood receded from his face, he let his head fall back against the chair to rest. "Nothing much. Just putting the world to rights with Matt." He struggled for breath. "Can't be seen to be telling them what to do, but he asked for an opinion, so I gave him one."

"So, how else can we put the world to rights today?" I asked.

"We probably can't. We are too old to have anything fashionable to say. We just have to watch them make their own mistakes. You look weary. Are you all right?"

He was the third person in a week to make comment on my health. I wished they wouldn't fuss.

"You're a fine one to talk. I hope you are taking something for that cough. I'm perfectly fit, thank you. Now stop fretting. Drink your wine and enjoy the sunshine. It'll be winter before we know it."

I really didn't feel too bad, at the moment. The only thing I had stopped doing much of lately was writing. I just didn't have the desire any longer – that burning need to get words out of my head and into written form was gone.

I'd never found euphoria where most people expect to find it, but then neither did the deadly lows change me. I'd never contemplated suicide. I'd had the emotional shot in the arm, the tears, the fears and the heartache, and survived; I'd been to the top and crashed to the bottom and still carried on. Through it all, my senses had been numbed.

I remembered the song put out by Peggy Lee in the late sixties called "Is That All There Is?" It became my signature tune and, like Peggy Lee, I kept on dancing – to whatever tunes were keeping the world spinning. I wondered how much longer either of us had. The rattle in his chest scared me. I didn't want him to die before me. Selfish, I know, but he would understand.

We discussed the latest book reviews in the paper and some of the new ideas he'd read about on the blogs.

"It's good I can talk to you about these things," he

said. "The others aren't interested in my book talk – except for Luke, of course. Linda tells me I'm past all that business now and shouldn't worry about it any more. I'm not worried, but I like to keep up to date."

I could see Linda saying something to Dave and Luke in the kitchen and looking at the two of us. I could almost hear their conversation in my head. They, too, would be worried about Michael.

"Hey, Dad," said David entering the room, followed by the others. "Hope you're feeling better today."

"Hello, son." Michael didn't comment further.

"Do you want a beer?" added Dave.

Michael shook his head and raised his wine glass to show he still had something.

"Can I get you a refill, Aunt Lottie?"

I handed him my glass.

Sharon stooped to kiss her father-in-law on the cheek. "I've got your favourite for dessert."

"Thank you, my dear," murmured Michael.

Luke shook his father's hand, laying his other one on top and holding the aged and frailer hand in his for a second longer. They had a special bond, those two, and understood one another. Luke then came and gave me a kiss on the cheek.

"Hello, Charli. Are you in a good mood today?" He grinned.

"Get away with you, you cheeky sod. Everyone else asks about my health, and you ask about my mood."

"You hate people asking how you are, and I want to know how to talk to you today. Shall I tease you, berate you for not writing, or console you?"

I knew exactly what he was talking about and gently punched him in the arm. Indirectly, he was asking which of my personas was occupying my mind. He wouldn't do any of those things, of course, not here, not in front of everyone else. The secret we shared belonged only to Michael, Luke and me.

"Bob's about to put the meat on the barbie but I think we'll eat inside tonight," said Linda, pulling the bi-fold doors closed. The temperature had dropped, and the evenings were closing in quicker since daylight saving had finished, so I was glad. I chilled easily. Michael did too, even if no one but me noticed.

A buzz of conversation filled the room while Dave and Linda took turns to check on Bob and the barbie, and Sharon and Linda set the table. Yet nothing in their discussions held any interest for me. Luke talked with his father, while I listened on the periphery hoping nobody would notice my silence. At one stage, Michael reached across and squeezed my hand to let me know he knew I was still there.

"I've steamed some vegetables specially for you, Dad," said Linda, putting the food on the bench top for serving. "I know you're not much of a salad fan. Help yourselves, everyone." She bustled across the room to help Michael up from his chair. She had started to fuss over him, and he didn't like it one bit but couldn't bring himself to tell her.

"Luke, you're not talking to Dad about book business again, are you? Leave him be, he's not well."

Luke resisted the retort I could see hovering on his lips. Instead, he meekly replied, "I didn't start it. You know it's Dad who asks *me* about what's going on."

Dinner conversation was lively, but Michael's involvement was minimal. When he did speak, he was succinct. At convenient breaks he chipped in with relevant comments involving the latest political scandal: "Someone's personal life is none of our business and shouldn't be discussed in the public arena. The press are just muckrakers these days." On the clampdown on home loans and how it would affect the younger ones starting out, he said: "I'll cover their house deposits. They won't want while I'm around."

When Dave began with moans and groans about people at work, Michael butted in to say, "You're sounding very mean-spirited." And when Sharon complained about a neighbour who had said something to upset them, he told her: "Stop being small-minded."

The criticism about how rates money should be spent displeased him further. "Enough of the NIMBY nonsense. Share your good fortune." But plans for Dave and Sharon's next cruise seemed to dismay him: "For goodness sake. Learn to love your homeland. New Zealand is a great country. It has everything anywhere else has to offer – and more. You should have made sure your children saw all of New Zealand before they, or you for that matter, spent money on overseas trips."

I expected them to argue or at least debate the issues with him, but something about the unreasonableness of his comments and the lassitude in his voice quietened them all.

"So how about some dessert?" Sharon got to her feet and started to clear the dishes.

Michael had barely touched the little put on his plate. I fared a bit better.

Suddenly four of them were gone, leaving Michael, Luke and I alone at the table.

"What was that all about?" I asked.

"I abhor the way people speak to and about one another these days. There's just no respect any more. I'm tired of the constant negativity about everything. I don't know what's wrong with people today. How can they find happiness in life if they keep coming up with something to complain about all the time? I'm just so tired of it all."

I raised my eyebrows. Michael was not his usual self.

"Don't stress, Dad," said Luke. "Linda is just being her normal, bossy, opinionated self, and Dave has always only thought about the status money brings. You won't change them."

Michael nodded and started to say something more, but another bout of coughing prevented any further comment.

"Are you all right, Dad?" asked Linda, pushing Luke to one side to pat Michael on the back.

Luke smiled at me. The Luke I knew was different, but in this environment, he held his peace. He was the most caring and understanding of souls.

Michael nodded, but I thought he looked defeated. "Stop fussing. I'm fine."

Dave refilled the glasses. Sharon placed a large sticky date pudding with a candle in the centre on the table, and Bob tagged along behind her with the jug of butterscotch sauce and tub of ice cream.

"It's present time," announced Linda as Dave handed over a large envelope. "Happy Birthday, Dad, from all of us. Well, except Luke, of course, who said he'd do his own thing."

Her criticism was uncalled for and I was about to say something when Luke put his hand on my arm. He knew it was a waste of time to argue.

The obligatory song was sung. Why, I don't know. At our age, we know what birthdays mean. Michael didn't even have the strength to blow the candle out.

"You shouldn't have gone to so much effort," he puffed.

"It's no trouble, Dad," said Linda. "There's a few vouchers in there. You can get some books or whatever you want."

Luke rolled his eyes. We both knew he could get Michael any book he wanted and often did. Michael didn't shop in the stores where he could use vouchers, but Linda would never think of that. She would think she'd given him choices.

"But on top of that we'd like to shout you a trip somewhere. We thought a cruise to the islands or around the Milford and Doubtful Sounds, if you like, or maybe a flight to White Island. What would you like to do, Dad?"

"You don't have to do any of that. The only thing I want I can't have."

Dave tried to jolly him along. "We'll come with you, of course. You won't be on your own. Come on, Dad. Which is it to be?"

"I really don't want to do anything like that. Not any more. Not without my Kate."

Stunned into silence at the mention of their mother's name, Linda and Dave looked at each other and then at Luke, as if he might have an answer. Dave shrugged his shoulders, but Linda looked like she would burst into tears any minute. She hid them as best she could by serving dessert before Luke could do or say anything.

"Here, Dad. Try some of this."

Michael accepted the plate and waited politely for everyone else to be served before he picked up his spoon. He sliced into the pudding, taking a little of the sauce and a touch of ice cream, then turned to me and whispered. "I'm sorry, Lottie. I love you. You know I do, but I love Kate more."

"Hush, you silly ol' codger. Of course you love Kate. You always will. What we have is something entirely different. Now eat."

Michael nodded and put the spoon into his mouth. Moments later he started coughing, his face turned red, his eyes bulged and he appeared to be choking. He put his hand to his chest and suddenly slumped forward, sending the plate flying. Linda screamed, Dave tipped over his chair as he stood up to get to his father, but Luke was faster. The rest of us stood back out of the way.

"Call an ambulance," I called to Bob.

"I will," said Sharon, fishing in her bag for her mobile.

Bob pulled the table away as Luke lay Michael's unconscious form on the floor in the recovery position. His face was very white and pulled up slightly on one side, but he was still breathing.

Linda knelt on the floor opposite Luke and took hold of her father's hand. Dave stood over them not knowing what to do.

"The ambulance is on its way," said Sharon into the silence. "It won't be long."

"Dad. Dad. Can you hear me? Hold on. Help is coming. Please, Dad, please. Hold on. Please ... Please, Dad. Don't die," Linda whispered over and over.

They had forgotten I was there – except for Luke, who had put his arm around my shoulders.

The ambulance arrived.

"I have to go with him, Charli. I'll be in touch."

I put my palm up to the side of his face. "Go. Be with him for me."

Tears pricked. Luke kissed my cheek and was gone.

They quickly and efficiently loaded Michael into the ambulance and drove off with Luke and Linda in the back. Dave said he and Sharon would follow in the car. Bob insisted he should drop me home before joining Linda at the hospital. "You can get your car tomorrow. You've had a shock, and that road is treacherous at night. We don't need to worry about you too."

I conceded. I didn't like driving at night and usually avoided it if I could, but I was never one to ask favours.

"Remember to let me know how he is, won't you," I asked Bob as I got out of the car.

"Of course. As soon as we know something for certain I'll get Linda to call you."

I watched him drive off, knowing I would never see Michael again.

*****

Emma arrived for her usual visit. I hadn't put her off despite the events of the night before. I was tired and cranky. I'd not slept well, but I didn't want to be on my own through the long day ahead. Even so, I was in no mood to talk or be remotely helpful.

The news from the hospital was what I expected: Michael had had a stroke, was in a coma and had pneumonia. The prognosis was not good. I chose not to visit him. I wanted to remember him at his best, not hooked up to machines and tubes to keep him alive. He wouldn't have wanted that. Neither did I. He wanted to be with his Kate, and the sooner they let him go, the better.

I remembered when Kate died – how inconsolable he was, how Linda and Dave tried to cajole him along to keep working, to keep active, to eat, to do anything other than sit and stare into the past. Steve had rushed home, clearly upset by his mother's death, but seemed to have no clue how to talk with his father. Luke was the one who had the knack with him and managed to know what was wanted.

I'd simply listened while Michael talked – as if I wasn't there – letting him relive his life with Kate in his mind and in his heart, where he was happiest. I never could understand why people think you must take your mind off heartache and tragedy if you are to recover. If anything, it is the other way around – to move forward, you have to make sense of it somehow.

"Morning, Charlotte." Emma sounded so cheerful, I felt my mood lift slightly to match. "How are you this lovely morning? I hope this sunshine lasts. I don't want winter to set in too early."

"I'm fine," I lied.

"I have a suggestion," she said. "If I offer to clean as I go, will you let me take the things from your cabinet and make some notes about them?"

"Only if you clean them properly," I answered churlishly. "There's silver cleaner in the kitchen cupboard, and use hot water and a good towel to dry things."

I let Emma open the china cabinet and take out all the little trinkets to get a closer look. I sat in my chair and watched. For the first time, I looked at them all through the eyes of a stranger and wondered why I'd hoarded so many useless items. The Amanda in me had kept them. The whimsical, wishful, hopeful Amanda who always believed something good would come from bad, and trusted people. Georgie was never that sentimental. I wish I could be more like Georgie.

Partway through the task, Emma pulled a faded black-and-white photo out from the back of the cabinet. My stomach flipped. I knew what it was, and froze. *Thank goodness, the original was hidden away*. Sitting on her haunches with her back to me, I couldn't read her expression as she held it in her hand staring at it for some time.

She stood up and brought it over to me. "You should put this in a frame. It's lovely."

I took it from her but didn't answer. I glanced at it briefly, knowing it was a photo of my mother when she was a child not long after World War I. I put it face down on the table beside me, trying not to show I'd got a fright. I'd forgotten it was there.

Years ago, Ray decided he needed a publicity photo, and when I wouldn't give him one, had taken the photo without asking and superimposed my signature on it. He copped an earful from me for being so deceitful, but I couldn't do a thing about it. He'd already printed and distributed them. Disgusted with him, I pushed the copy he'd given me out of sight to the back of the cabinet. From then on, I never trusted him and stored all my photos in a locked wooden box in my wardrobe, well away from prying eyes.

Swearing silently under my breath, I could only hope Emma hadn't seen a version of it anywhere, but something about the frozen look on her face and her voice rang warning bells.

"Enough of all this old stuff, I think. There's nothing here that'll help your story," I snapped and hauled myself out of my chair. Gingerly, I knelt on the floor in front of the cabinet and started putting everything back into place.

"What are you doing? I haven't finished." Her voice held an edge of panic.

"Doesn't matter. Just put that cleaning stuff away and leave the past where it is."

She shrugged her shoulder and pulled a face but did as she was asked. She returned to the living room and even helped me put things back again. I slowly got to my feet, smoothed the front of my unfashionable but comfortable long skirt I wore around home and sat down again, feeling suddenly weary.

"I've got enough information about your early life now anyway, so can we look at the next phase of your career?"

She sat on the sofa opposite me and opened her notebook. "Tell me about what it was like when you came to New Zealand. How old were you?"

"Twenty-one."

"Did your parents come with you? Your mother?"

"No."

Emma's surprise was obvious. "You travelled alone?"

"Yes," I lied. Emma would never ever know who travelled with me.

"What did you do after you arrived?"

"Not much."

The look she gave me was severe. "Could you expand a little and give me more details instead of me asking all the questions?"

"No. You ask. I'll tell you if I want to."

Her eyes changed and her mouth hardened into a challenge. "Very well. Tell me about that autographed photo. The one of a little girl wearing a bangle."

That photo is going to be a problem. "No." I closed my eyes.

"Why not? Is it you?"

I could not and would not answer. Some secrets I had to keep. "It's not relevant to the story," I answered. "Next?"

Although clearly frustrated, she had the good sense not to pursue the topic. Instead, we entered into a question and answer session.

"Where did you live then?"

"In a boarding house."

"So where was your china cabinet while you lived there?"

"In storage." She didn't pursue any possibilities there either. Thankfully.

"Where did you work?"

"I was a Girl Friday for a music agency."

"Why such menial work when you had so much talent?"

I opened my eyes to look at her. I shrugged.

"Why didn't you return to the stage? Or singing. Record some songs, or, come to think of it, write for the stage or something like that?"

I shrugged again.

"Oh, for goodness sake!" She shut her notebook with a bang and thumped it down on the table. "This is getting us nowhere. What do you want to talk about, if you won't answer my questions?"

"Not my life."

"All right. Your first book was published forty-five years ago, which is why Ray wants a bio of your lifetime achievements. But if my calculations are right, you came to New Zealand around 1959 or 1960. What did you do in that nine-year gap?"

"Wrote down my thoughts."

"Thoughts about what?"

"My life."

"But you won't talk about your life."

"No."

Emma stood up, picked up her notebook and handbag and headed for the door. "I'll come back when you're in a better frame of mind."

I heard the door slam behind her. Something I would have done in my younger days. I understood her frustration, but else what could I do? If we followed that path, I might let something slip and I mustn't lose control, never mind what the provocation.

*****

I remember only too well the day I arrived in Auckland. The ship steamed up the harbour one February morning as the sun shone on the glistening water. I'd never seen anything so beautiful as this place I was coming to.

I'd convinced my fellow passengers, the shipping company, the immigration people and other officials that I was either: a young woman travelling to New Zealand to meet her husband, who was waiting for her at the wharf; or an abandoned wife – or a widow, as necessity demanded. After all, I wasn't an actress for nothing. One thing I could do was lie. The only thing I brought with me from my previous life was my mother's china cabinet and its treasures, finally claimed from the lawyers and safely stored waiting for its new home in New Zealand.

The day we arrived was my twenty-first birthday. With me, I brought a new life – and the chance to forget my past and create another new me. Except it wasn't to be. Britain was shaking its conservative attitudes by the late 1950s and heading into the wilder, free-spirited and heady social freedoms of the sixties, influenced by music and drugs. New Zealand had yet to embrace the change. A married woman without a husband by her side was a difficulty, but a single woman with no man to guide her was a disaster. I invented a life for each situation, which at least gave me a place to live and a bank account.

But Emma was asking questions, digging up a past I'd hoped never to speak of again. I didn't want her to know. I was no longer ashamed of what had happened to me back then, but I was not the same person either, and I didn't want her, or anyone else, to know that person – that vulnerable, frightened and desperate young woman.

*****

The phone rang.

I knew without picking it up what the voice on the other end was going to tell me.

I had lost the last person I had ever cared for. There was nothing and no one left for me now. I knew what would happen next, although it could take some time to kick in. I have no control over my response to upset and tragedy. My reactions are deep-seated, repetitive – and crippling. Either I would be struggling with the nervous, can't-sit-still internal flutterings of impending doom that would have me rushing about gabbling nonsense to break the silence, or a leadenness of spirit would drop over me, distancing me from life and wrapping me in a fog of confusion full of indecision, lethargy and tears, and unable to move from my chair. Maybe Emma's nagging would help this time and keep the worst at bay.

Emma had wanted to know what I did in those nine years between arriving in New Zealand and publishing my first book as Charlotte Day. I'm not sure I wanted to tell her the reasons, but I wrote. I wrote as Georgina Strong, long before I wrote as Charlotte Day and even longer before Amanda Grove crept into my life. I just didn't publish them until much later. I wrote about the harshness of life, the insensitive, undignified and inhumane treatment of people by those who thought they knew best – the doctors, the lawmakers. I wrote about injustice.

I remembered too well the confused and disturbing images of injections that burnt into my arm, my leg, my buttock, wherever they could get purchase to stop my out-of-control panic attacks, my ungovernable explosions of anger, to stop me self-harming, to calm me down. They shovelled pills into me until I rattled, until my mind was so foggy I could hardly recall my name – or which name.

They still want to shovel pills into me. But no more. I am going to take control of what happens to me next, whatever that may be. I'll die on my own terms.

Emma

What is it with that woman? Just when I thought I was making progress, she shuts down and refuses to talk to me. What the hell am I going to do now? What is it about that photo?

I'd invented the perfect excuse to empty the cabinet and found what I'd wanted. Except it wasn't the original I'd hoped to find, but a smaller copy of the signed publicity shot I already had. So what's its secret? I still don't understand. Who is in the photo? Damn and blast. This is so frustrating. I'd wanted some sort of response I could work with, but she says nothing. Is it of her, or just a random image Ray conjured up? Maybe I should ask him - but I probably wouldn't believe him, if he told me. I don't belief half of what he says already. He's so fond of blowing his own trumpet that everything becomes his idea and nobody can do anything as well as him. If I showed any interest in a promo shot, he'd take credit for piquing my curiosity. That's the whole point of them, but I didn't want to puff up his ego any more.

Thanks to Charlotte's constant chattering about her mother, I am thinking more about my mother and the life she led. I'm trying to find truth in the details she fed me through her bitterness. Most of it I ignored, with typical teenage angst – anything a mother had to say had no bearing on my life. But now I've started to think about the things she said.

Maybe Charlotte's ideas about how a child is raised have merit after all. Despite my denials, I have to admit how much of my past I've brought into my present. I just chose to reject my mother's teachings and did the opposite.

Last night, as I lay tossing and turning, I remembered more things and wondered about the parallels in my life to that of my mother's. I got up early and started to write it all down, all the similarities and all the nuances, trying to find the hidden link. I wanted – needed – to make the connection with my mother's past.

I tossed around names, dates and hidden messages and drew a blank, but I knew we were hiding behind a smoke screen of names, like Charlotte with her pseudonyms. I've done the same, keeping my maiden name to hide the disasters of my married name.

But there was something else. I just couldn't put my finger on it.

Charlotte

May

"Hello, Charlotte. Are you in a better frame of mind today?"

Over the last three months or so, I'd learnt Emma didn't beat around the bush.

"I am what I am, thank you. And don't push your luck, young lady."

"Ah. So, you *are* feeling better; two sentences in a row and irascible. Perfect."

I laughed silently, not letting on I was amused or that she was right. In one way, I did feel better. The pain had eased for now, and I had been looking forward to her visit. It seemed we were like two peas. Similar, but different: each enjoying the company of the other. "I'm glad you used such a wonderful word," I said. "I'd have been disappointed in a lesser description."

Now she laughed.

We sat in the lounge overlooking the garden, glad of the sunshine. Summer had gone and although autumn had been wonderful, it would soon be time to retreat to my snug. I could already feel the chill seeping through the windows when the evenings drew in, even though it was still early May.

"So what would you like to talk about today?" she asked.

"Michael."

"Michael? Your old editor guy, you mean? Why him?"

"He died."

"Oh." The look on Emma's face was a picture to behold. She obviously thought I would talk about my life, but now she knows Michael has gone, she doesn't know what to say. I wonder how much she knows about death. The young often don't.

"Ah, yes," she flustered. "I'm sorry to hear that. I didn't know him, of course. Do you want to tell me about him?"

"I might." I paused. When I had her attention, I announced, "I want you to take me to his funeral on Friday."

Emma turned white, then green. Her eyes glistened, her jaw dropped and her mouth opened. Just as I began to think she could be having a heart attack or I'd mysteriously injured her in her some way, she spoke. "I can't," she stammered. She nervously shifted position several times and tugged her skirt down to her knees. "I don't go to funerals." Her voice was stronger – and determined.

"Too bad. You are coming to this one."

"I am not." She sounded jittery. "There is nothing you can do or say to make me."

"How about no more talks and no more stories if you don't come with me?"

"I'll manage," she flustered.

"No, you won't. You badly want my story for some reason. And it'll eat you up if you can't get it."

"Like I said, I'll manage."

"I don't believe you."

Emma got out of her chair and strode into the kitchen. I could hear the tap running.

"A lot of people will be there," I called out.

She didn't reply.

"Bring me a glass of water, there's a girl. And come back in here where I can see you."

A minute or so later, she reappeared carrying two glasses and sat down opposite me. She'd regained her composure, but her mouth was set in a hard line. I didn't think it would take much to push her over the limit and get her angry.

"Michael was well respected in the industry. All his old cronies – at least those who are still alive – are bound to turn up, but more importantly, so will the ones who followed him. You might even meet people who remember me," I said, casually dropping tempters into the well of persuasion.

"Why do you even want to go? You hate crowds. You told me so yourself."

"To pay my respects, of course."

She scoffed. "You don't mean that. The only reason people go to funerals is either to be seen or to show support for the family. The dead person doesn't know you're there, and the ones left behind need more than empty words. You don't want to just 'be seen'," she snarled, miming the speech marks. "So what support will you offer? I can't imagine you helping anyone cope with loss."

Oh, my. What an outburst. Looks like I've hit a sore point. I had deliberately antagonised her so I would not take offence at anything she said, but I couldn't let her off the hook completely. "Thank you for that charming vote of confidence," I replied, my voice sharp with sarcasm. "I seem to recall many of my stories are about loss, so I think I do know what I'm talking about."

We sat and glared at one another as the minutes ticked by. I waited to see what else she might burst out and say. She desperately tried not to say anything but, as with a staring game, one of us had to concede. She caved in first.

"You didn't answer my question. Why do you want to go?"

"Because."

I'd done it! That one word released the explosion I'd expected and waited for.

"Because why? you manipulative old cow. Ray told me you were, and I gave you the benefit of the doubt, but he's right. What are you up to? There is no reason you need to go to this funeral – you can make your excuses to his family, and they will understand. I can't comprehend why you want me to go."

"Because until you face life head on you can't write about it. You have an opportunity in front of you to be a writer. But you don't even see it. And to be a writer, you can't hide."

"You do."

"I do now. I couldn't back then, which is why I started to write. Which is why I can write."

She left me then, without a word. Just gathered up her things and walked out. I wasn't surprised by her reaction, but she'd be back. She would take me to Michael's funeral, and I would go, with every fibre of my being screaming. Emma was right; I didn't want to be there. I didn't need to be there, but I would do it. I would go because I saw me in her, and I didn't want her to end up like me. If that meant I had to be a bit of a bully, so be it.

At times of stress, the events of my early years resurface and linger in my thoughts. Every birthday – mine, my mother's and one other very special birthday in my life – every Christmas and every anniversary, they all remind me of the stories yet to be told.

*****

The day the Auckland Harbour Bridge officially opened, 30 May 1959, was the most important and eventful day of my life, and the day the girl known as Rose-Anne Thomas lost her most precious possessions. The day when a decision, made against my will, would influence the rest of my life.

How can I ever explain? I can't even justify it to myself; I only know that day tipped me over the edge into the anger, confusion and heartache that has never truly left me. I thought I was beginning a new life. Instead, they took a new life away from me.

"What do you mean, you are taking her away?" I squeezed the tiny bundle in my arms tighter.

"Come along now, we've been through all this." The matron was a no-nonsense sort of person with hard features and an absolute belief in the righteousness of what she was doing.

My heart hammered in my throat, and the feelings of desperation and loss I'd felt when my mother died attacked in full force, leaving me stammering in their wake.

"No, no. Leave her be. She's mine. She's all I have. You can't ... you can't take her." Tears streamed down my face and my nose was running, but I wouldn't let go to wipe either away.

"It's best for baby. You shouldn't have been allowed to hold her in the first place," said matron, glowering at the two nurses, even though it hadn't been their decision.

I'd been caught in a web of my own making. Tom *had* abandoned me as soon as he heard about the baby, so I hadn't been entirely untruthful, but neither was I a wife or a widow, despite my pretence to the contrary. For that reason, I'd used the name Charlotte Day to travel to New Zealand. I wanted to continue my new life in my new country without any links to the past, but my legal name remained Rose-Anne Thomas. I didn't understand when I used that name to register for a midwife and the authorities realised I didn't have a husband, that my baby would be taken away from me. I signed forms that had not been fully explained. They promised me I would be looked after, they would help me find employment and they would give me a home while I waited for the delivery. Afterwards, I could never work out whether they said taking my baby away was punishment for my sins or that I was a wonderful mother for giving her away. Either way, they took her, and they might as well have taken my heart too.

"Miss Thomas, you are behaving irrationally," said Matron, who was fast reaching the tip of her tolerance. "Now stop being difficult and let the nurse take her."

"Will I be able to see her?"

"Of course not! Think of the harm that would do to the child."

"What about the harm to me?"

"You should have thought of that earlier," she snapped back with malice.

"But what will I do without her? She needs me, I'm her mother."

"Once she goes to her new home she will have no need of you. She will have a real mother and father who will love her and care for her."

"But surely ..."

"No. Stop arguing. It is the law. You cannot have anything further to do with her. An adopted child is to have no knowledge of her birth mother. Nurse, take the baby."

It took two nurses to prise my arms from around my little girl. I struggled and screamed but in the end had to watch one of them hurry away holding my child, while the other held me back, whispering soothing sounds. She disappeared through the door and her footsteps faded into the distance down the corridor. My heart shattered, my spirits plummeted, and only Georgie was there to comfort me.

Emma

"I don't care what you say," I yelled at Ray. "I'm not going."

I didn't quite know how Ray and I had got into this argument. I'd arrived back from Charlotte's, tense and filled with dread, to find him already ensconced in my living room.

"Now, sweetie, don't be like that," he cajoled, turning on the smarm.

I hated the way he called me sweetie. I may have willingly got into a relationship with him at the beginning, but his increasingly ingratiating bullying tactics of late had really got up my nose. I wanted rid of him, especially now he'd somehow got into my place when I wasn't there. That scared me. I was on edge and, in my heightened state of self-preservation, I knew I was right not to trust him. He had to go.

"You know she wants us both there to fly the flag for her," he continued. "What's so bad about it? I didn't like the old man any more than he liked me, but there you have it: the harridan wants it and she always gets what she wants."

"Not this time she doesn't," I snarled adamantly.

I would not survive another funeral. "Anyway, why would she want you to go? I thought she'd fired you."

"Oh, she does that all the time. She doesn't really mean it."

I didn't believe him. He might pretend to himself he was still in charge, but Charlotte thought otherwise.

"What are you doing here?"

"I came to see you, of course." He moved a step closer and put out his hand, but I backed away. I didn't like the creepy feeling raising goose bumps on my arms, and I was in no mood for his style of inducement.

"Bullshit. You want something – and it isn't me. How did you get in?"

"It wasn't hard – you left the ranch slider unlocked."

Alarm bells rang. I was certain I had locked it before I went out. It was second nature. I never deadbolted myself in but left the key in the lock so I wouldn't lose it. It was unlocked now and slightly ajar – and the key was missing. When did he take it? And why hadn't I noticed?

"I think you'd better go."

"Not yet, sweetie. We need to talk."

"About what exactly?"

"Just what do you think you are up to."

He said it calmly enough, but the thudding in my chest warned me we were getting into dangerous territory.

"What do you mean by that?"

"All little miss innocent, aren't you. I had my suspicions about you, so I took my chance to have a good look around this place. I did a little digging and had a talk with Jacqueline. You are not who you say you are. I want to know what you are up to, and I want a piece of the action."

"Jacqueline? Who's that?"

"Don't you remember? Your editor friend. That's who."

"I don't have an editor. I told you I work freelance," I challenged, hoping to play for time to think.

"You know exactly who I mean: the Jacqueline who pays your wages. She isn't as distrustful as you. Jacqueline was happy to hear from me after so long, remembered me fondly, in fact, and was glad you had been in touch. Poor girl, she said, such a sad history. She wanted to know how we were getting on and how your exposé about Charlotte Day was coming."

I didn't want him knowing about my past – he'd find nothing he could hold against me or threaten me with, but I didn't trust him. I had done nothing wrong. I was the injured party, the unhappy victim, the lost soul trying to hide from myself. What could he do to me that hadn't already been done?

"So, now you know? So, what?"

"What's your little game with our dear friend Charlotte?"

"I have no idea what you're talking about."

"I think you do. You came to me begging to do an article about how a publicist worked, promising me an exclusive in the magazine if I went with it. But now I find out not only is there no exclusive, there's no money either. You knew I wouldn't agree to anything without payment. Why did you so desperately want to meet my most famous client?"

"What does it matter to you?"

Suddenly, he was standing over me, millimetres from my face and gripping my arm so tightly I knew it would leave bruises. His anger was barely under control.

"If you think you can wheedle your way into getting Charlotte to sign any deals with you, you can think again. She's mine. She's my moneymaker, so you can go find your own pot somewhere else. Anything she gives you, anything she tells you, is mine. Understand?"

Just as suddenly, he let go of my arm, smoothed his suit jacket back into place and turned on his charming smile again.

"So, back to Michael's funeral. You will go, as I will, because I say so. You will smile and be charming and supportive, and I won't tell her what a lying, cheating little reporter you are. She hates reporters with a vengeance, and if she thinks you're going to write a sensational magazine article on her, she'll throw you out faster than the leftovers on her plate. See you tomorrow."

The door closed quietly behind him as I stood in the middle of the room wondering how I'd let myself get into this predicament. Tears started to fall, and I crumbled to the floor feeling my strength desert me.

I didn't care what he knew about my past. Ray Morris was unimportant, but I couldn't let him destroy what I'd built up with Charlotte. I needed to know her story. She was right: it was eating me up, and something about it drove me to get up the next day.

Charlotte

May

The whole funeral thing had left me drained. I let everyone think the emotion of losing Michael had caused my collapse – and it was, partly – but it was more than that.

The minute I opened my eyes sometime in the predawn, I knew the day was going to be difficult. The additional trauma of going out, smiling at people and saying goodbye to my friend would make it all that much harder. I drugged myself up heavily before Emma turned up at my door, as I knew she would.

Ray phoned. "Let me take you. It will look better if I escort you. You shouldn't appear alone. We should show solidarity and support for each other at this trying time ..."

"No. I don't want to go with you."

He blustered and puffed that I shouldn't think of driving myself, never for one moment thinking I might have already arranged something. Stupid man.

Blah, blah ... I stopped listening. He's become impossible. And I thought I'd fired him.

I ignored it all.

"Don't let me stop you if you want to go, but don't go on my account. You don't work for me any more, remember."

When Emma finally arrived, she didn't look much better than I felt. She was immaculately dressed again in a suit and blouse with her hair pinned back, but her jawline was tense. She constantly clenched and ground her teeth together, setting mine on edge in the process. The dark shadows under her eyes told me she'd either not slept or had been crying – or both. I would talk to her about it later, when I could, but we had a chore to do first.

The trip to the church was conducted in silence.

To my surprise, Emma stuck by my side the whole time. She held my arm as we walked into the church, remaining silent while I spoke to Michael's family. Linda was putting on a brave, tearful face but remained fully in charge of proceedings. Her eyes wandered to check everything was as it should be. Dave said he accepted his father had been old and ill, and his passing fitted the normal ebb and flow of life. Steve, jovially catching up with old friends and acquaintances, explained he wouldn't be staying long as his wife and kids were back in London. Luke looked desolate.

"Thanks for coming, Charli," he whispered, hugging me close. "What are we going to do without him?"

"Continue as before, as he would have wanted," I answered. Luke squeezed me tighter before moving on to other well-wishers. He would cry in private, I knew.

Emma guided me to a pew, sat beside me, opened the hymnbook to the right page before I even had a chance and never looked right or left, nor spoke to anyone during or after the service. I hated being in church, unable to believe their mantra about everything happening for a reason, making us stronger through adversity. None of it made any sense to my life. Maybe she sensed my distaste, or maybe she had her own reasons for her obvious discomfort.

Even as we wandered into the hall for sandwiches and cakes, she made no effort to talk to anyone. I pointed out several people and told her what their role had been, reminding her I'd promised she would have the chance to talk to some of them about me. There were people who knew me from my younger days when I went to book signings; a former subeditor who had worked closely with Michael, and even a fan who asked when my next book was coming out. They all spoke to me, but Emma only nodded, murmuring a polite hello when good manners forced her to. She bristled tension and held herself rigidly upright and clung to my arm, only leaving my side long enough to get me a cup of tea and a plate of sandwiches. She neither ate nor drank.

I don't know whether it was the tea that caused it or not, but after the first mouthful a shot of lightning tore through my abdomen. I lurched forward, dropping the cup and unceremoniously toppled onto the floor, scattering hot tea, plates and sandwiches in all directions. Emma immediately bent to help me as Ray flustered about pretending to be doing something other than getting in the way. Linda and Luke rushed over to see what the noise was about, closely followed by Dave. Apart from the indignity of it all, I was unhurt and unwilling to let on about the pain.

"I'm fine," I assured them as they helped me to my feet and seated me back in a chair. "I was a bit overcome that's all. I'm finding it too warm in here with all the emotion. I'm okay. Linda, go do what you have to. Don't fret about me. You go look after your girls, Dave. They look like they need you." Amanda and Chelsea, who must be well into their mid-twenties, loved Michael as much as he loved them.

Luke wanted to call an ambulance. "Just in case. I don't want you suffering from shock or anything like that."

"No, no. There's no need. I just need to lie down. Emma will take me home now. Come see me, when you can." He helped me to the car despite my blustering that Emma could do it perfectly well by herself.

The return trip was also conducted in silence beyond the necessary polite enquiry as to how I was. The explosion would come, I thought; she couldn't hold it all in like this for much longer.

"Thank the stars that's over," I said as she helped me inside. My legs had gone wobbly, and I could feel the sweat popping out on my forehead from the pain that had now settled everywhere. I hadn't wanted her to see me like this, but it didn't look like I had much choice.

"Pour us both a large glass of red wine, will you. I think we need it. I'll turn on the heat pump, and we can sit in the snug."

"What's wrong with you?" she asked moments later, handing me my glass. "You look terrible."

"Humph. Thanks for the compliment."

I looked at her for a few seconds trying to decide whether I should tell her or not. She'd thrown off her suit jacket, untucked her blouse and unpinned her hair, which had grown surprisingly long over the months, and let it fall naturally over her shoulders. She looked young, vulnerable.

"We need to talk," I said.

"Go on then," she said, gulping down a huge portion of the wine in one go.

"I think you should tell me your story."

Emma looked at me sharply and drew her lips between her teeth. "What story?"

"I don't know what it is, but it's destroying you."

She shrugged, shifted awkwardly and tried to sound as if none of it mattered. "Two can play at that game. Why should I tell you anything when you are so determined to keep your own secrets?"

I raised my glass to her. "Maybe if I drink enough, I'll share a few. *If* I think it will help."

"What if, like you, I only answer the questions I want to answer?"

It was my turn to shrug. "Then you'll never shift that massive iceberg in your heart, and life will continue to be the empty space you think it is!"

The guffaw rattling the back of her throat almost choked her as she swallowed another gulp of wine.

"You have no idea about my life, so how can you judge what I think?"

"Because I've lived a long time in this world, because I observe people, because I know what life did to me, and because I see me all over again in you. Will that do for starters?"

She stared at me for several moments. I could almost see her thought patterns as she debated whether to admit to something or not.

"Okay, so life isn't a barrel of laughs. So what? Who can say they are truly happy?"

"Michael was – until his Kate died. After that he settled for one tier less and found contentment in his children and grandchildren."

"Yeah, well. If you have a family, that might work. More wine?" she asked, draining her glass as she stood up.

I shook my head. I'd hardly touched mine. I watched her pour another generous glass.

"What about you?" she challenged as she sat back down and kicked off her shoes. "Are you happy?"

"I am ... or rather I'm content. I like my life. I enjoy what I do. I love my garden, my roses and the peace and solitude this place gives me." As I said this, I realised it was true, now. It hadn't been once, but somewhere over the years I had found some inner peace.

"Ray calls you a crabby old witch."

She raised her eyebrows – goading me to react.

I simply laughed. "Does he now? I'm not surprised. He makes me crabby. The only reason I put up with him is because he sold my books." I took a sip of wine.

She was restless, constantly changing position, fiddling with her hair or biting the side of her nails. I wondered how I was going to get this conversation going on a different tack. "How old are you?"

She stopped fidgeting for a moment and answered automatically. "Thirty-three ... Why?"

"Just thinking about where I was and what I was doing at your stage of life. Do you remember your grandparents?" And remembering I wasn't in any better space then either.

"No. I never had grandparents. My grandmother died before I was born and my grandfather when I was about four."

"That's a shame. Grandparents tend to spoil their little ones or so I've been told. Michael did. Looks like we both missed out there. I didn't have any either. So, where did you live when you were a child?"

"Here and there. Wherever Jinny took me?"

"Jinny?"

"My mother. She hated being called Mum, said it made her sound old. She was always Jinny – short for Jennifer, and I know – before you say it – I know. Jinny is not normally short for Jennifer, but she wanted to be different. She was different. She was an artist. Rather a skilled one, I realise now."

"Go on, tell me about her," I urged, noting she used the past tense: my first clue.

"She was tall, flamboyant and colourful. Your eyes remind me of her. She wore her hair long and braided, and was very creative. She could sketch in charcoal and paint with water colours equally well, and she made fabulous jewellery. She designed and tie-dyed her own clothes and a range of skirts and harem pants to sell."

So she admired her mother even through her hostility. "And your father?"

"Nope. No father." She swallowed another slug of wine. "Jinny always had a bloke but never any that stayed around for long. She'd shack up with them for a while, make some things she could sell, then we'd be off again. She loved the gypsy life."

I kept my face as emotionless as possible, in the hope I wouldn't betray how distressing I found her story. But she'd given me a second clue to her life. I went on questioning her about the unimportant things: the colour of her mother's hair – fair, like her; where she went to school – home-schooled apparently; and her favourite subjects; the things she liked to do; her friends. I emptied my glass; she emptied the bottle and opened another.

I asked her to make us a sandwich and coffee, hoping it would soak up some of the alcohol. I barely ate mine. Neither did she. I swallowed more pills and hoped she was too caught up in her own problems to notice mine. The pain was getting worse.

The afternoon slipped by. The tension drained from her face, her restlessness eased and she even laughed occasionally. She talked about the crazy times she and Jinny had with science experiments going wrong, or seashore study walks and getting trapped by the tide. Funny moments, memory-making moments.

We talked about books we'd both enjoyed, a movie and other memories of the good times. I told her about life in the sixties and seventies, hoping it would add colour to her picture of her mother.

"My memories include Kombi vans, paisley print and geometric patterns, especially on the ubiquitous Crown Lynn china, bright colours and polyester. I wore flowing skirts similar to those of your mother's that you described. I didn't have the courage to wear the mini. I always thought my legs were too long and too skinny."

"I would kill for legs like yours – and hers," she said.

"You're not that much shorter than me."

"I felt it when I was young."

"That's normal. We never like ourselves when we're young. Sometimes we don't like ourselves much when we get older either, but that's another story. Now, what else? Long hair, Babycham, cheap sparkling wine, but we didn't know any better in those days. Hm, The Beach Boys, The Monkees, the Wahine disaster, Whina Cooper and the land march. Know about them too, do you?"

At last, I'd made her laugh.

"Of course! I remember having to write essays on the last two. I used to love writing stories – even when I was little. English was always my best subject, and Jinny encouraged me to look and really see what was around me and tell its story. It was her idea I become a journalist. I think she figured it was a way I could earn money from something I enjoyed."

Darkness settled and she suddenly announced she was starving. She promptly jumped up and started rattling around in my kitchen, raiding the freezer and pantry, throwing together a stir-fry from what few ingredients I had.

"That was delicious. Sorry I couldn't eat more," I said, after I'd cleared less than half the plate. I hoped it would stay down. "Where did you learn to cook like that?"

"Had to really. Jinny couldn't cook to save herself. If I wanted to eat, I needed to learn."

She looked relaxed, and I felt my chance had arrived. "She's dead, isn't she?"

Emma tensed, her hands curled, and tears of misery welled in her eyes. Biting her bottom lip again, she nodded. The customary condolences rushed into my mouth, but I decided they were not the right things to say. She didn't want sympathy; she wanted to make sense of it.

"It's tough losing your mother," I acknowledged. "There's something illogical about it. It's rough at any age, but more so, I think, when you're young."

Emma nodded again, although I couldn't quite gauge her reaction. She was bent over looking down at her feet, and her hair had fallen forward, shielding her eyes.

"Is that why you didn't want to go to Michael's funeral?" I queried. "Scared it would bring back memories?"

Another nod.

"Now I understand. We share quite a lot really. I had no one at your age either. No parents or grandparents. Just me, alone against the world."

A scratchy whisper, muffled by her hair, reached me. "How old were you?"

"When my mother died?" I hesitated. Should I tell her? Why not? I thought. What did it matter now anyway? "Fourteen."

I heard the intake of breath as she sat up and flicked her hair behind her ears. She looked at me in silence for a few moments.

"You were hardly more than a child. Who looked after you?"

"I looked after myself!" I sounded far too indignant and felt I should justify my words. "In those days the laws were different. I was put into a foster home but I left the home and school the day I turned fifteen and headed into the world."

We chatted about some of the jobs I had, how music and getting into the theatre had directed my life. I talked about Mrs Sweet, my old landlady, about life on the ship coming over and the miserable boarding house I'd lived in when I first arrived in Auckland. I painted a picture mostly of fun and laughter, all carefree and full of optimism. I left out what I didn't think relevant – the pain and heartache, the uncertainty and gloom, the pregnancy. I also left out my sense of guilt. I knew I'd turned myself into a cold, hard-nosed creature only capable of emotion in my books and I was still scared of letting go, but something about Emma brought out a side of me I didn't know existed. I wanted to protect her.

She'd listened intently, nodding occasionally, but said nothing. "Writing has been my outlet ever since. So, there you have it. My secret life."

When I'd finished, she just sat there, looking at me, then she started to giggle. Absurdly. I had no idea what I'd said that would cause such merriment, but the laughter grew until she was almost hysterical with it. Tears streamed, and she wiped her face with the back of her hand like a child. And still she laughed.

I got unsteadily to my feet, passed her a box of tissues and rescued the newly poured glass of wine that nearly got knocked over.

"What on earth has got into you?" I demanded, quite shaken by her uncontrolled emotion.

"Secrets …?" She sounded incredulous. "Secrets …? You call those secrets?" Her uncontrolled laughter had her gasping for air before she could speak again. "Is that all you've got? That's your 'secret' life?" More laughter. "They're not secrets. You have no idea," she gabbled, her voice steadily rising throughout, and promptly burst into distraught sobs.

I gave her a glass of water, made her swallow one of my tranquillizers, wondering whether it was a good idea with what she'd drunk, but decided it was worth the risk. I took another painkiller and sat down again.

For a while, neither of us said anything. She finally stopped bawling, developing hiccups instead, and began tearing the tissues to shreds in agitated fingers.

"Drink some more water. It'll help the hiccups."

Emma obediently did as I suggested and finally controlled her breathing until it was back to normal.

"Do you want to talk about it?"

She shook her head, picked up her glass of wine and took another gulp.

"I think you've had enough, don't you? And you'd better sleep in the spare room for the night. You're in no fit state to be on your own, and I will not let you drive anyway."

Silence again. She finally nodded. "I'm sorry. I don't know what came over me. I'm really sorry. I shouldn't burden you with my problems. Oh, I'm so embarrassed."

"Shush, now. We'll talk some more in the morning."

I led her along the corridor to her room and shut the door on the forlorn figure perched on the side of the bed.

I'd recognised the pain of loss in her eyes.

*****

I'd been at the boarding house I'd checked into when I first arrived in Auckland for only a few weeks when my waistline suddenly expanded and I could no longer hide my predicament. The landlady had eyed me disapprovingly, knowing I did not have a husband around, and suggested I move on.

"I don't want the likes of you in my establishment. Thank you. You have until the end of the week."

I hadn't argued. It wouldn't have mattered to her what my story was. I didn't have a man to take charge of me, so I was an embarrassment. I ended up living at the Bethany Home waiting for my time, helping with the cleaning and the laundry and whatever other menial jobs they could find.

I hated the matron from the first time I met her – and have done my entire life – but I couldn't blame the nurses for what happened that day. They were as terrified of the old battle-axe as I was and would have lost their jobs for not obeying orders, but neither could I trust them.

After they took my baby away my milk came through, but with no little person to feed, the pain was intense. Not that Matron cared.

"You'll just have to put up with it until the body learns you have no need for it, and it will dry up naturally."

I was lucky the midwife was a warm-hearted, cuddly and, most importantly, kindly person who became my friend and ally. She bound my breasts, which helped the pain, but nothing filled the emptiness. Music had helped colour the void after my mother's death, but nothing could fill the vacuum that was blacker than the darkest night after they took away my child.

All I could do was cry until I was exhausted.

*****

I thought I would not sleep. Emma had stirred too many memories and the pain of the afternoon had not left me, but eventually I must have dozed off. I awoke from my restless dream still sitting in my chair where I'd returned instead of going to bed. The timer had turned the heat pump off, and I shivered in the cold early hours, despite the blanket wrapped around my legs. I got up, put the kettle on and took some more pills, wondering what the day would bring.

Maybe I could keep my condition from Emma for a while longer. She was so upset last night I don't think she noticed my discomfort. My ill-advised ploy to get her mildly drunk, hoping she would open up and talk to me, only worked in part. I had found out some things, but they were mostly what I'd suspected anyway, and I'm certain she's on the verge of a breakdown. She's still holding on to her secrets, thinking my secrets could not be as bad as hers.

I wasn't sure there would be any point telling her about my Rose, as I named her. Only a mother can truly understand what it is to love a child so absolutely, and only a mother who has lost a child can truly understand the magnitude of that loss, never mind how hard anyone might try. Emma wouldn't understand at all.

I'd need to steer her back to life in New Zealand in the sixties and hope it distracted her enough. She likes talking about her mother even if she denies it to herself.

"Is that tea you're making?" Emma's voice startled me. She'd found the towelling bathrobe I always left hanging behind the door, but not the hairbrush. Her hair was awry and she looked like a lost child.

"What are you doing up? It's still the middle of the night, girl."

"I needed the bathroom, and I'd kill for a cuppa. I'm dying of thirst."

"I'm not surprised." I threw a teabag into a second mug and poured the hot water in, pushing it across the bench towards her after I'd squeezed the tea bag out.

"What, no teapot? I'd felt sure you were a teapot person."

"Usually I am, but not at this time of night."

I took my mug and sat down again, wrapped the rug around my knees and reached for the remote control for the heat pump. I must get the garden man to set the fire in the coal range. I would need it soon.

"How are you feeling?"

"Embarrassed."

"No need. You just had one too many wines after an emotional day. Chalk it up to experience."

"Have you had any sleep?" she asked, peering at me over the mug she clasped in both hands.

"Not much. But then I don't need much. It's one of the lesser joys of old age." I hesitated. "Are you okay? You were very upset last night."

Emma shrugged her shoulders and dropped her head.

"Do you feel you could talk about it? If not to me, then someone who could help you?"

Her head moved from side to side, her hair swaying around her face, but I didn't think she was simply saying no. She seemed unsure of what she wanted.

I softened my voice. "I know what it's like to be alone, and it takes a long time to come to terms with it. Let someone help you," I urged, suddenly feeling ridiculously sentimental. I knew I was stepping into territory that was none of my business and she may not thank me, but she needed help.

I drank my tea listening to the night sounds above the gentle fan of the heat pump. The house creaked.

"Charlotte. If you don't mind me asking – why did you never marry?"

She took me by surprise. Did she want to change the

subject back to me or make comparisons? I wondered if I did mind the question and decided I didn't.

"Lots of reasons. Lack of opportunity – New Zealand men scared me. The country didn't come by its rugby, racing and beer culture by accident – but mostly because I preferred the make-believe worlds I could create to the real world."

My real world, when I might have been thinking about marriage, made it impossible. I didn't want to tell her about my dark days. They still haunted me, and while I'd mastered them now – mostly – I didn't want to relive my time shut inside brick walls in case I remembered too much.

She chuckled then, throatily, but with a hint of her normal self. "Jinny used to complain about that too. She said the only thing men thought about was 'The Log of Wood' and how much beer they could drink."

"My goodness, 'The Log of Wood'," I echoed. "I haven't heard that mentioned for years. The Ranfurly Shield was a huge tournament in its day. The rivalry over which of the provincial teams would win the trophy was intense – not that I knew much about rugby. Still don't understand it. But I do remember the six o'clock swill."

"The what?"

"That's what they called it," I explained, as she took the empty cups and put them in the kitchen sink.

"The men would pour out of their workplaces and head straight to the pub to guzzle as much as they could before it closed. I couldn't believe such a thing existed, coming from England where pubs shut at ten or eleven, but here early closing had been around for decades – since the First World War apparently. It caused a lot of trouble."

"I can imagine," she muttered, looking around the kitchen. "Can I have a biscuit or something? I'm hungry."

"If you can find any, but make yourself a sandwich if you want."

She hunted the cupboard for biscuits but only found some crackers. After popping one in her mouth, she put the sandwich ingredients out on the bench and started to butter the bread.

"Do you want one?" she offered.

"No thanks," I said, carrying on with the story. "The women were the ones who got the worst of it. The men either spent all their wages, leaving nothing for the rent or food, or she'd get a beating if she said anything. Domestic violence was common and, unbelievably, not against the law."

"Truly? I'd give back as good as I got if someone started bashing me!" She took a bite out of the sandwich and brought it back with her to the snug to finish.

"It wasn't as easy as that sounds. The laws didn't favour women. Anyway, the swill ended in sixty-seven, thank goodness, and not before time from what I could see. Pity the binge drinking didn't stop. By the looks of what I read these days, the young ones still do it. It's just so unnecessary."

"You're right. There are far too many fools who think drinking until you can't remember anything is a good night out. I like to drink – as you have seen," she added guiltily, "but not to that point."

"You aren't alone," I said, admitting my liking for a good glass of wine. "Oh ... listen."

We sat silent, waiting to hear the call of the morepork again.

"I'm beginning to like the remoteness of this place. I like the sounds of the bush," said Emma. "I don't think I've ever heard a morepork so clearly or so close before."

A few more moments passed as we kept listening for other sounds: the rustle of trees, even the silence was mesmerising.

She eventually broke the spell. "What was it like – everyday life – back then?"

There wasn't much I could tell her, I thought. I had no family, so life for me was different anyway and often lonely.

"It was more about family life, I suppose. People made their entertainment at home with the whole family – grandparents, aunts and uncles, cousins – everyone lived close. Playing cards, talking, a sing-song around the piano. A day out to the beach was the highlight of the summer months, picnics and Sunday roasts. At least that's what Michael and Kate used to do. Life was much slower back then.

"I can't imagine what that would have been like," she said wistfully. "These days we rush everywhere at a mad pace and are always on the phone or the Internet."

"I've noticed. In those days, a postcard was all you'd get if you were lucky. The most nostalgic fact I can trot out is that we would leave our doors unlocked and windows open, and hardly anything ever went wrong."

"So why were your make-believe worlds better places to be? They weren't all about champagne and roses. There were harsh times in those worlds too, especially those of Georgina Strong. Why did you decide to use a pseudonym – and who *is* Georgina Strong?"

"Digging for dirt, are you, my girl?"

"Not at all."

I wasn't sure I entirely believed her, but we'd both mellowed in the months since she'd first arrived on my doorstep – become almost friends. She was not so belligerent and determined, and I was not so scared of the truth. Not now Michael had gone. Not now my days were numbered. What did it matter any more?

"I'm just curious to know how and when you decided to be someone else," she said, sounding genuinely interested. "What prompted you to write under a different name?"

Emma shivered, tugged the bathrobe closer and pulled her feet up under her.

"Go get yourself a blanket from the cupboard in the hall if you're cold."

"I will, thanks. Back in a mo', so don't think you can avoid the question."

I didn't intend to avoid it completely, but she had unwittingly given me the perfect opening. If I gave her a rundown on the sixties, I could hopefully distract her from my state of health and those missing years she kept on about.

She sat down again, wrapping the blanket around her like a shawl, and curled up in the chair.

"Firstly," I began, "you have to understand society was changing dramatically and quickly in the sixties. The first TV broadcast brought with it a whole new world. People could get the news from overseas instantly, watch the Olympic Games when Peter Snell and what's-his-name Halberg both won gold in athletics. Tourists and immigrants started arriving by plane as well as by ship. Medical and space technology was at its height with heart transplants and then the moon landing in sixty-nine."

I was getting into my stride now I had a captive audience.

"But more importantly, it was the era of rock and roll. The Beatles and The Rolling Stones even came here on a tour. The world was opening up to quiet old New Zealand, and people were discovering a newer and better life – with supermarkets, shopping malls and even new money. Decimal currency was introduced in sixty-seven, but you're not old enough to know anything about pounds, shillings and pence anyway. I bet you don't even understand feet and inches."

Emma shook her head. "No, but I do know about Snell and Halberg, and the moon landing, and you forgot to mention the electricity cable laid in Cook Strait in sixty-four to provide the North Island with power. Jinny was a great teacher in those early years," Emma defended. "I remember us making a mobile of the solar system out of beads and Ping-Pong balls. "

"Good to hear it. So, in that case, you should know the bad things about the sixties – the assassination of both Martin Luther King and John F Kennedy, the Vietnam War, drugs and the pill."

"The pill? Why the pill? Surely that was a benefit to women?"

"To married women who didn't want to be pregnant every year, yes, but it fostered promiscuity and sex for the sake of sex."

"Fancy that. Such a terrible thing to do," she said, sounding deliberately prim. "Sex instead of a bunch of unwanted children."

"Enough of the sarcasm, miss."

"You asked for it, sounding so prudish when I know you're not."

"If the abuse statistics are anything to go by, we've still got more than our share of unwanted children. People shouldn't have kids if they can't look after them."

"Ah, yes. You have a point there, I suppose. But I don't think the pill has anything to do with that."

I shrugged. I often say things I don't necessarily mean, just to provoke an opinion.

By this time, the tea had done its trick, and after the sandwich she had a bit of a sparkle in her eye.

"But you've forgotten to tell me about Radio Hauraki, the pirate radio station that took to sea to broadcast from outside the three-mile limit - or something like that - so they could play the rock music that had been banned. Let's see, mid-sixties I think. Kiri Te Kanawa won the Mobil Song Quest about that time, and *C'mon* on TV launched stars like Ray Columbus, Maria Dallas and John Rowles. Um. Have I missed anything?"

Now it was my turn to laugh. She had caught

me out being smug and superior and had played the hand back to me. I should have known she would be well informed.

"Touché," I said, reaching out to give her a high five, something I'd learnt from Luke. I felt a deepening respect for this girl who could play me at my own game.

"You've just reminded me about a funny story to do with Radio Hauraki's boat, *Tiri*," I said, wrapping the blanket around my knees again. "I knew this bloke back then, a teacher he was. He was down at the wharf the day the *Tiri* planned to sail. The police turned up in force, and there was a bit of pushing and shoving between them and the crowd. Anyway, this bloke was one of a group trying to lift the ropes off the bollards. When he looked up, he saw his brother, who was one of the policemen, pulling on the rope from the other end. The police were trying to keep the rope taut so the protestors couldn't cast it off. It doesn't sound much in the retelling, but I found it amusing. The brothers were engaged in a literal tug of war over a social matter. It's in one of Georgie's books somewhere, but I dramatised it a lot more."

"I like how Georgina writes about that sort of thing," she said. "Social change. Your first book, as Charlotte Day, came out in 1968, which, by the way, is where I found out all that stuff about the music scene. Georgina didn't appear for quite a few years after that. Why? Or rather, why not? What drove you to write as Georgina Strong?"

She was wrong in one sense. Georgie came first – I just didn't publish her until later.

"Books don't just appear," I said. "I started to write about life in New Zealand not long after I arrived, but I couldn't get the voice right. Barry Crump released his book *Good Keen Man* about that time, and I knew then I could never capture that outdoorsy, Kiwi manner. I played around with it for years but never published it."

"Have you still got it?"

"Not sure. Probably not. I figured people didn't want to read about a life they were living, so I picked on stories about a world I did know about – the music world. The theatre was a glamorous place to go in those days. People dressed up for it. I figured it had an aura of mystique that would appeal to readers.

"I worked as a secretary-cum-girl Friday with a talent agency and got to know many of the performers. I knew about life backstage, the middle-of-the-night sessions, the tiring rehearsals, the performance buzz, and wrote fictitious and not-so-fictitious stories about it."

"Didn't you ever want to return to the stage?"

"Strangely, no. I'd lost my confidence or my desire. Not sure which, but it wasn't the same. The music was different. It was rock and roll, not stories with music. The wonderful new musicals like *Oliver, Hello Dolly* and *Fiddler on the Roof* hadn't made it here. If I'd stayed in England, things might have been different, but I hadn't."

"Those early books of yours were mostly about success and fame or failure and loss. None of your heroes found love and romance."

"That's what life was like, as I knew it. You were either top of your game with everything at your fingertips, or out of work, out of luck and out of here, as the saying goes. The music industry was a tough one. There was no time for love."

"And Georgina? What about her?"

Another pain stabbed my lower back – deep, persistent. At a time when she was perking up, I was paying the price for my night in the chair. I glanced at the clock – it was still short of five o'clock.

"That'll have to do for now I think, Emma. Help yourself if you want a shower. You'll find everything you need in the bathroom. Stay or go as you wish, have some breakfast. I'm going to lie down and see if I can catch up on some sleep."

"But you haven't answered my question."

"Another time. Maybe."

Emma

I hadn't stayed. I'd wanted to get back to the flat and add to my notes while everything Charli'd said was still fresh in my mind. I'd been a bit surprised when she started to become Charli in my thoughts. I hadn't liked the name Lottie – it was old-fashioned and sounded wrong for this woman who could be fearsome and impressive in equal parts – but Charlotte was too formal. I needed something warmer, more familiar – something personal. Charli seemed to fit.

I found a large pad and drew up a timeline of what I did know. Birth, arrival in New Zealand, first book by Charlotte Day, books by Georgina Strong and Amanda Grove. I filled in the death of her mother, her theatre performances, where she'd lived. I didn't know when her father disappeared from the scene. Did he die? Or did the parents separate?

Eventually, I sat back and stared at the page in front of me. Something was missing. Something about her bugged me, but I just couldn't put my finger on it. I had more than enough to write a series of magazine stories, and I'm certain she'd guessed that, so why was she letting me stay on and why couldn't I let go?

More than six months had passed since Jacqueline had given me this task, and while I'd managed to give her some articles from the list of other 'has-beens' she'd handed me, I'd done nothing on Charlotte. Jackie had not complained or given me any grief until I phoned her about Ray.

"How dare you!" I yelled into the phone. "How dare you tell that slimy creep anything about me?"

"Do you mean Ray? He said he was worried about you, and I agreed. I'm worried too."

"He wouldn't know how to worry about anyone except himself."

"Well, I've been worried. I've no idea what you've been up to. You've hardly kept in touch since you left Wellington. I thought it would help you if someone else knew."

"Well, it didn't. He's an arrogant, controlling bastard."

"He is egocentric, I'll give you that, but he's good at his job."

"Bullshit. He's a bully. He drives Charlotte to distraction."

"Are you getting too pally with this Charlotte? You need to keep an unbiased head on your shoulders. I want stories that will sell. The others are okay – just – but you're losing your touch. And I want some dirt to work with."

"You're changing the subject," I growled.

"Listen to me, Emma. Right now, I pay your wages so you'll do things my way. I've been more than patient. I understand what you're going through ..."

"You can't possibly know what I'm going through."

"Well, maybe not exactly, but ... you need to get a grip on reality. Get some more counselling, take some pills or do some digging into your past to find what you're looking for. I don't know. What I'm trying to say is that I've been as understanding as I can and given you heaps of leeway, but no more. I need you to write something decent. I can't just keep on paying you and getting rubbish in return."

"Well, don't then. I quit. This time I really quit. I want Ray Morris as far away from me as possible and the quickest way to achieve that is not writing anything about Charlotte Day."

I slammed the phone down and burst into tears. They seemed the one constant in my life, the tears. The counsellors told me that anger would help: anger would burn up the tears and give me focus. That anger would pull me out of my despair. They were wrong.

I holed up in my apartment and let myself remember, let the pain back in and thought about what Jacqueline had said. Did I need more counselling? Or should I dig into my past? The past I hadn't cared about. The past Jinny had kept hidden from me. There were so many things I didn't know and didn't understand.

Losing my baby girl, my Ruby, was the worst thing that had ever happened, but at least I could almost understand it. I could understand she'd contracted a horrible disease and died because of it. There never would be any answers to the 'Why me? Why her?' questions that constantly echoed in my brain, but babies die from illness all the time, and every parent asks the same questions – but she didn't have a choice.

What I didn't understand was why Jinny left me. She did have a choice: she chose to die.

Charlotte

I hadn't been surprised to find Emma gone when I finally got up, but I was surprised to find no message from her, and, as the day wore on, no calls asking to visit again. I was worried, seriously worried. I'd seen that look in her eyes.

Against my instincts, I resorted to asking Ray.

"How should I know? She spends more time with you than me."

"She's not answering her phone. Have you had any luck?"

"No, and there was no reply when I went round to her flat earlier. Dunno where she's gone."

There seemed to be nothing more I could do until she resurfaced. Damn this disease! I should have stuck it out and kept her talking. It was only pain. She's in pain too. Only her pain is different. I shouldn't have forced her to come with me to Michael's funeral. It was too much for her, but I didn't know that until after.

Why the hell should I care? It's not my place to look after her, never mind how much I want to. I know I've pushed and pulled her in all directions, trying to get her to face her problems, so she doesn't end up embittered like me and what does she do? She runs away and hides – just like I used to.

Why should I care?

But I was amazed to find that I did.

"Miss Day," said my doctor sternly the next day. "You have been ignoring all the advice I have given you."

"It's not going to make me live any longer so why bother?"

"It could. If you would only have treatment you could get months more, maybe up to a year, but you are running out of time."

"No. I won't have treatment. The only reason I'm here is for more painkillers. Stronger ones if you have them. I'm nearly seventy-seven for goodness sake. Another few months isn't going to improve my life one iota."

"You must stop drinking at least," she instructed.

"Why? I enjoy my glass of wine. It's the only thing that still tastes any good."

"It will hasten things."

"I'll manage my death the way I have managed my life. On my own."

"Isn't there anyone who could help you?"

"I don't need help."

"You will. You will need someone. Do you want me to arrange for some home help?"

"Just give me the damned prescription and I'll be on my way."

She gave up, tapped a few keys on the computer,

printed out the prescription I'd asked for and showed me out the door.

"Horrible woman," I muttered, as I drove away from the chemist with a new bottle of pills in my bag, annoyed she'd pointed out the obvious and inevitable. I would have to plan my pending mortality after all. For once, Georgie couldn't help me.

One thing I was determined about, I wanted to see my roses bloom one more time. I had reached the end of my life cycle just as this season's roses had reached theirs. The full-blown rose was barely hanging on and the petals littering the garden were being blown about in the wind. The difference was the roses would bloom again. Their life would continue season after season. Mine would not. There was no one in my likeness to follow me.

I decided to start pruning them right away. It was too early, the wrong side of the shortest day, but beggars can't be choosers. Every day for a week, I got out and pruned a bush or two. I got angry. Frustrated I couldn't do as much as I wanted, but determined not to ask my garden man to do it. I needed to do it all myself, perverse as that sounded, even to me. I'd let him tidy up and get rid of the prunings later, after I'd finished.

Every day I would come inside to rest and think about Emma, and every day I phoned her and left another message.

Every day I became more concerned.

Every day I remembered.

*****

I could sense Georgie sitting on the bed beside me, stroking my brow where the electrodes had been. She was always there to comfort me. I hated the shock treatment, standard practice for depressed, unmanageable people in those days, but it took away the sharp memories that haunted me in the lead-up. I could never forget, of course, but the shocks removed my short-term memory and made life more bearable for a while.

It had taken years to reach the point of such despair, but losing my mother, my father, my baby, my country and my identity had finally got too much, even for me. I'd cracked and found myself crying for no reason. A heavy weight settled on me, and everything became too hard, every decision seemed like a mountain to climb. I buried myself inside a cave of my making. I stopped going out. I couldn't go to work. I stared into nothingness until I thought my head would burst from the pain.

Eventually, a doctor sent me to this place where I recovered. I went back to my life, until it happened again and I returned.

The last time in the outside world, I thought I'd been doing well. I'd felt so much stronger, but then her birthday had come round again and I remembered I was alone. Anyone who had mattered to me had been taken from me. As a result, I never allowed myself to get close to anyone, to reveal anything, afraid if I started to trust again, it would destroy me.

Georgie began telling me I was better now. I could be who I wanted to be and leave the past behind me. I didn't need these people any more. She wouldn't let it go. On and on she went, day after day, month after month, until finally I believed her.

"Miss Thomas?" a voice said. "Miss Thomas," the voice repeated.

I was sitting in the garden, studying the roses, as the gentle breeze rustled the leaves on trees over my head. I'd watched those roses grow and develop, bloom and fade and bloom again. Nothing stopped their cycle. The sprinkler watering the lawn oscillated back and forth beside me, missing me, but as I watched it, I wondered if it would change course unaided and I would get wet. I stared blankly at the man in the white coat and wondered whom he was talking to.

"Miss Thomas, you asked to speak to me."

Slowly, I remembered where I was, who I was and what I was doing here - again.

"I've been told you wish to discharge yourself."

I nodded.

"I can't stop you, of course, but I do recommend you stay for more treatment."

I shook my head.

"You've been in and out of here several times over the course of quite a few years. Are you sure?"

I nodded. He and I had had this discussion before and been over it all. I knew what I had to do to get better. I wasn't going to change my mind. Just like that sprinkler. It wouldn't move from its path unless someone moved it. Neither would I.

"Very well, if you insist. Your treatment has been successful overall. I see from your notes your panic attacks have receded, as have your fits of anger, and I think the ECT treatment may have cured the disruptions in the brain that caused it all. Has the writing therapy helped?"

I nodded again.

"Tell me about it?"

I cleared my throat, moistened my lips and swallowed hard. I wasn't certain I could speak, but I heard a voice that sounded like mine.

"I've learnt to put my feelings onto my characters, and I use other names to write my stories, so it's not me. I use several names and sometimes I can forget who I am. That way I detach myself. The things that upset me no longer happen to me, they happen only in my stories. It works for me." I had it all off pat, just as the therapist had told me, knowing it was my escape route.

"Good. The drugs should keep you feeling on an even keel. Don't hesitate to come back at any time if you feel you are losing control."

I left Oakley Mental Hospital and Rose-Anne Thomas behind for good that day. She ceased to exist. Charlotte Day never looked back. Georgie was right.

*****

I remembered too well sliding into the pit of despair; I couldn't let it happen to Emma. I had to find out what had happened to her. I just had to.

I swallowed my pride and phoned Ray. "Where does Emma live?"

"Why do you want to know?" He sounded wary.

"I haven't heard from her for days. I just want to know she's okay."

"She'll be okay. She'll be packing a sad, you made her go to the funeral."

"In that case, I need to apologise. But she isn't answering her phone."

"Let me try. Or I can go round instead if you like and let you know what she says." He sounded too enthusiastic and something didn't ring true.

"I thought you said you'd already been round to her place?"

"Um ... Did I? No ... I don't think so. I think I said I would if you wanted me to."

That wasn't how I remembered it. "Don't give me bullshit. Just give me the address. I want to see for myself."

An hour later, I pulled up in front of her unit. It was at the back, underneath the front house, with its own entrance on the left-hand side. I knocked on the door, noticing Emma's car was parked on the lawn as if she'd just arrived home. There was no reply. I knocked again and called out her name. I could feel the jitters mounting. Something wasn't right here. I walked around to the back garden and looked through the ranch slider from the small paved area.

I breathed a sigh of relief. At the far end of the room, I could see Emma curled up on the sofa with her back to the light, fast asleep. I knocked again as loudly as I could and called her name until I was shouting but couldn't budge her. I wondered if she had taken a sleeping pill.

That thought had barely crossed my mind, when another more worrying thought flashed through it. How many sleeping pills and how long had she been like this?

I punched Ray's number into my cell phone.

"I need you to help me break in to Emma's place – something's wrong. Get here as fast as you can. I'm going to call an ambulance."

I hung up, pressed the emergency button and was put through to the ambulance service. While I waited for them, I tried shouting through the glass again but nothing roused her. I cupped my hands around my eyes to get a better look but she'd not moved. I looked to see if she'd hidden a key somewhere but could find nothing for either the ranch slider or the front door. I'd resorted to pacing by the time Ray arrived.

"What's your problem, Lottie?" he asked as he climbed out of the car.

"Don't park there, the ambulance is on its way. They'll need that space, but hurry. You'll have to break a window or something to get inside."

"All right. All right. Stop panicking. You don't know what's wrong. Here's the key to the ranch slider. Let yourself in. I'll shift the car."

I grabbed the key from him and trundled as fast as I could back to the door, even while I wondered why he should have a key and what it meant. The key turned in the lock and although I managed to slide the door open enough to let a cat in, it suddenly jammed. I looked down to see a broom handle stuck in the track. Damn!

Ray arrived by my side then. "What's the matter? Why can't you get in?"

"She's blocked the track."

He muttered something under his breath. I got the gist. He wasn't pleased.

The ambulance arrived before I could quiz him about the key. The young male officer asked a barrage of questions to help him decide what to do next, while the other officer collected a bag from the rear of the ambulance.

"What's the person's name?"

"Emma Wade," I replied.

"I'll just see if I can rouse her first," he said.

Seeing the door slightly ajar he reached his hand inside, banged on the wall and turned on the light. He then rattled the door and called out her name a few times. Whether it was the change in tone, the deeper voice or the fact the door was now partly open I don't know, but Emma changed positions.

"Emma. Can you wake up for me, please?" he said again slightly louder, knocking on the wall inside. "Emma. Can you hear me? Emma?"

She moved again, rolled over, nearly sliding off the couch in the process, and jerked into wakefulness. Putting one hand to the floor to save herself, she put the other up to her eyes to shield the light.

"Emma, don't be startled. I'm from St John's Ambulance."

Looking anxious, she put her hands up to both ears at the same time and appeared to pull something out of them. She got to her feet and hurried across to the door, bending down to remove the broom handle, then opened it wide.

"What's wrong? Why are you here?" she asked, looking bemused as we all stepped inside. She looked very young to me, dressed in bright blue PJs covered in cartoon animals.

"Your mother was worried about you and called us."

"My mother?"

"Yes, this lady here," said the young man. "Isn't she your mother?" He looked at me sceptically as if I'd committed some sort of crime.

"I'm sure I can explain ..." I began.

"Never mind that now," said Emma. "What's all the fuss about?"

"She couldn't wake you."

"Oh. No. I don't suppose she could. I took some sleeping pills and put earplugs in to shut out the noise. I can't sleep without them."

"What time was that?"

"Um ... I couldn't sleep so I got up around two and tried to do some work. So it must have been around four this morning."

The second paramedic wrote down some notes. "Did you take any before you went to bed last night?"

"Yes. I've not been sleeping well, and I just needed something to knock me out, but they didn't work."

The two ambulance people glanced at one another, obviously noting the double dosage.

"Can I just check your vital signs, please ma'am, now I'm here. To make sure you are okay?"

While the officers did their routine checks, Ray leant against the kitchen bench pretending to be occupied with his smartphone, and I sat beside Emma nervously working my hands round and round, wanting to touch her but afraid she would reject me.

The immaculate young woman I had first met was nowhere to be seen. Emma looked dishevelled, her hair hung loose and was in need of a wash, her face was pale and pinched, and her legs spasming with nervous agitation while she sat.

A few minutes later, the young man cleared Emma. "Everything looks fine, so we'll be on our way. But a warning - do not take more tablets than prescribed."

"Thank you, officer," I said, rising to go to the door with him. "I'm sorry it was a false alarm. I'm so sorry to have wasted your time - I do appreciate how valuable it is."

"The office will send an account, but no call-out is a waste. It could have been something serious. We're pleased when it is not. Have a good day."

"Can someone tell me what is going on?" demanded Emma with sudden acerbity. "And what's he doing here?" she added, pointing to Ray.

"Oh, Emma. I'm sorry. It's my fault. I was worried when I didn't hear from you. I couldn't get you on the phone, and when I saw you lying unconscious on the couch, I panicked. I asked Ray to help me break in, and I called the ambulance."

"But I wasn't unconscious. I was just trying to sleep." She appeared to be on the verge of tears.

"It didn't look like that to me - I knocked and called and you never moved. It was just lucky Ray had a key, otherwise we'd have had to break a window."

"I told you a spare key would come in handy," said Ray, with his false smile, reminding me of a grinning fox.

She jumped to feet and her rage exploded.

"How dare you! Get out. Get out, right now," she yelled at Ray.

"Sweetie. Don't be like that."

"I've told you, don't call me sweetie, and don't ever come round here again. And I want my key back, you asshole."

"Not until I get something sorted between the three of us."

"Among," I said automatically, hoping to take the edge off the rising tension.

"Pardon?" Ray looked at me as though I'd gone mad.

"You say between when it's two people and among when it's more."

"You're crackers, you old has-been, but I already knew that. Among. Between. Who cares? I want my share of whatever you two are cooking up *between* you. You can't shut me out of it. You have a contract with me, Charlotte Day, and you are not to deal with anyone else."

His face had turned puce with rage. I, on the other hand, now Emma was okay, felt totally calm.

"I think you'll find, Mr Morris, that I decide what you have a share of and what you don't. One thing Michael was very careful about was protecting my interests. Check the contract. I fired you and repeated it again last week. You get a one-off payment as per the contract, too generous in my opinion, but that is all. Goodbye, Mr Morris. Thank you for your services. Now piss off."

He glared first at me, then at Emma. "I'll get you for this, you bitch," he spluttered.

"Which of us is the bitch?" I asked quietly. "Just so I'm certain, when I talk to my lawyer."

"You can't get rid of me that easily. I'll ... I'll ... fix you."

"Mr Morris, let's be clear," I added, hardening my tone. "If you breathe one word against me, my books, my characters, or my associates – Emma included - in any shape or form, I'll sue that expensive suit off your duplicitous body and reduce you to ruin. And don't think I won't."

He stormed towards the door.

"Just a minute," snapped Emma. "I want my key."

"It's all right, Emma. I've got it," I reassured her, as Ray kept walking.

Emma sank into the couch and rubbed her hands over her face. The image of vulnerability and despair I'd seen before settled over her.

"I'll make you a cup of tea," I said, heading towards the little kitchen at the other end of the room.

She lay down on the couch, adjusted the cushion under her head and closed her eyes.

"Do you want me to go too?" I asked.

"No. Stay. I'd like the company."

I made the tea, carried it over to her and put it on the side table, but she didn't open her eyes. I quietly turned the armchair around so I could sit closer and watch her. I felt quite shaken by all the drama. I hadn't driven so far in a long time and had forgotten what Auckland traffic could be like.

I waited, nursing my cup in my hand while I took in the room. It was too impersonal, even fully furnished. There were no photos, no magazines or books, and no knick-knacks of any kind to give me a hint as to her background. The tartan rug carelessly thrown to one side over the arm of the couch didn't strike me as a personal possession either. On the floor beside the couch lay a scrapbook and a couple of notebooks, one closed over a pen leaving it partly open, and a cardboard file box, all stacked in a pile. She was obviously working on something before she fell asleep. What time was that? Why had she slept on the couch? And why sleeping pills?

Sitting still in the quiet, I had time to let my nerves settle and admit that I was exhausted. The nagging pain raised its vicious hand and stabbed me a couple of times; my head was bursting and nausea filled my throat. It unnerved me to think how weak I was becoming.

Just as I was thinking Emma had fallen asleep again and maybe a visit to the bathroom and a peek at the bedroom might satisfy my curiosity, she spoke. "You must be wondering what this is all about."

"Can't say I haven't thought about it," I hedged.

She sat up then, swept the hair from her eyes and took a swig of her tea. "That would be an understatement, if I ever heard one." She drank the rest of her tea in one go, wiped her mouth with the back of her hand and leant against the arm of the sofa, tucking her feet up beside her. "If nothing else, the writer in you should be taking notes to use in a story. You are dying to know more about me. That's why all the questions before I embarrassed myself totally."

"I thought it was the other way round," I contradicted. "I thought it was you who wanted to know about me. Isn't that why you turned up at my house all those months ago full of charm, bravado and questions? I'm just wondering what happened to that confident young woman compared to the one I see before me now."

A hint of a smile flicked at the corner of Emma's mouth. "It's nothing. I'll be back to my normal self before you know it. I told you I don't like funerals."

She didn't convince me. Things didn't add up.

"Have you been inside this flat since then?"

"Yes."

"Doing what?"

"Nothing much." She shrugged and tucked her hair behind one ear.

"What's all that paperwork down there on the floor?"

"I was putting your story together."

"So why didn't you answer my phone calls?"

She stared at me, her face a blank while she thought up an excuse.

"Have you been ringing me? I didn't know. The battery must have gone flat."

"And you didn't notice? You, who lives by your phone!" The questioning inflection in my voice should have told her I didn't believe her.

"I got engrossed with my work and forgot. All right? I'll charge it now."

She got up then and looked in several places before she found her phone still in her handbag, carelessly thrown on the floor beside the sofa.

"I checked your fridge earlier – there's no food."

She began to plug her phone into the charger on the kitchen bench behind me.

"So what?" She tried to sound dismissive but came across as rattled. "I haven't had time to go shopping, that's all. Did you want something to eat? I can go and get you something."

"No. I'm not hungry." I snapped, feeling decidedly light-headed. "I want to know why you shut yourself inside this flat for days on end, ignoring the outside world, and why you felt it necessary to take enough sleeping pills to knock yourself out sufficiently that you couldn't hear me banging on the door. Never mind what you told that paramedic. You took more than you let on."

"What's it to you what I do?" she snapped back at me, her face flushed as she looked down at me, daring me to argue.

"Because ..." I searched for an excuse, not yet willing to let on how concerned I was. "Technically, since I fired Ray, you work for me, and you haven't finished your job, and I want my pound of flesh."

"Ha! Now we're getting to it. As long as it suits you then everything is hunky-dory, but we mustn't inconvenience the famous author now, must we?"

"Good. Get mad at me. I don't care. I want you to face up to whatever is eating you up and has been ever since you arrived on my doorstep, young lady. I'm tired of all the leading questions and innuendos. You've not written a single word, so what do you want from me?"

"The truth!" she flared, eyes blazing.

"What truth?"

"The real story behind Charlotte Day and her pseudonyms."

"I'll trade you," I retaliated without thinking. "Tell me why you took those sleeping pills."

"Why did you tell the ambulance people you were my mother? No way are you my mother."

"Can I help it if the paramedic made the wrong assumption?" I lied.

The steam suddenly went out of her as fast as it had erupted. She resumed her position on the sofa and turned her head away. She seemed to want to hide from me all the time.

"I wasn't intending to kill myself, if that's what you were thinking. I'm just desperate for sleep – a real, long, long sleep. I haven't had much of that for years. Not since ..."

The unfinished sentence hung in the air.

"Since your mother died?"

She nodded. "And ... ah ..." She didn't finish that sentence either. Who else had she lost? A husband? A sibling?

She sat silent, still avoiding my eyes, and stared out the window. I recognised that look, the one that rolled back the years to end up in a different time and place.

"Tell me about the photo," she asked in a voice as distant as her mind.

Should I? Could I? It would open a can of worms and I didn't know which path they would take and, worse, I couldn't be certain I wanted to find out.

"What photo?"

She spun upright and banged her feet on the floor with angry intensity. "For f ... Pete's sake ... Charli, you know very well which photo."

Impressed she'd modified her language, especially since she was so upset, I wondered why? Could it be out of respect for me? Respect was not so common these days that one could take it for granted, but I made no comment and picked on something else that shocked me.

"Charli?" I repeated. Only Luke had ever called me that. How did she know about my pet name? I tried to sound annoyed. "Charli? Where did that come from and what gives you the right to think you can call me by that name?"

"Sorry, I didn't mean to let it slip," she said, immediately contrite. "It's a nickname I gave you since I've been working on your story. You weren't supposed to find out. You wouldn't have if you hadn't made me cross with you again."

"Humph. Now why would you be cross with me? Ever, let alone again," I acted the innocent even though I knew exactly what she meant.

"Agghhh," she growled as she got to her feet and paced around the room. "Because you deliberately provoke me. Like now."

"I don't provoke, I question. It's your conscience that chafes at you." Just like mine had chafed me all my life. I could fool her - and others maybe - but never myself. I knew my foibles too well.

"So tell me! For pity's sake, stop procrastinating and tell me," she cried and sat down again.

I gazed at her intently, reading her body language, her facial expression and the strain swamping her.

"First tell me why you so desperately want to know. It's just a promo shot and a stupid one at that."

Emma bit her bottom lip, dropped her head into her hands and said nothing. Several moments passed before she raised her head and looked at me. "Because ... " she choked.

She bounced to her feet and disappeared into the bedroom. A few minutes later, she reappeared with her hands behind her back until she stood centimetres away from me. Slowly she withdrew her arms and extended them before her. I took the two photographs from her outstretched fingers, surprised to find my hands shaking. One was the black-and-white promo shot with my signature scrawled across it. The other was an ancient sepia photo and an exact copy of the original I had hidden in my box at home. Memories came rushing back, my mind desperately tried to put dates and places into order and failed in the storm of emotions raging through me.

No wonder she wanted to know. So did I.

In a ragged voice, she said, "I knew I'd seen the photo before but couldn't remember where. Talking with you about Jinny sparked my memory. I came home and found it in her things. Jinny always said it was of her grandmother." She paused. "How did you get a copy of it, Charli? I don't understand the connection. Who is she?" Her voice was barely above a whisper, and tears were trickling down her cheek unchecked.

I stood, intending to wipe them away, but a fierce pain swept through me. I staggered and fell into the dark centre of a multicoloured vortex that opened up and swallowed me.

Part Four

The past, the present and the future

Charlotte

July

"Stop fussing, Emma, dear. Please."

This battle of wills had been going on for over a month now – ever since my ridiculous collapse at her feet. I had no recollection of it at all. I woke up in the hospital with tubes sticking out of me and a stern physician telling me my behaviour was foolish. He wasted his breath of course. I had no more intention of listening to him than I had my own doctor. I knew the consequences of my decision, but I was sticking by it.

What had changed was my acceptance of Emma as my companion and caregiver. What an ugly word that is. I hate it, but despite my extensive knowledge of the English language I hadn't been able to come up with anything better.

Just like the paramedic, the hospital had assumed she was family and had allowed her to sit with me while I lay in an unconscious state. The two photos, modern and old, side by side haunted my disembodied mind. What did they mean?

It didn't take Emma long to work out what was wrong with me, given all the admonishments and instructions being handed my way as soon as my eyes opened. The hospital insisted if I was going to refuse treatment, then I needed daily, in-home care as a minimum to start with, and maybe more. They were in the process of organising professional help, but I was having none of that. I didn't want strangers in my house, poking into my business, asking inappropriate and meaningless questions and remonstrating with me.

As I lay in that miserable hospital bed wondering how to beat the system, I made another decision: one that would prove life-changing for me, and for Emma – I hoped.

"Why are you here?" I'd asked, one afternoon when she was visiting and the doctors and nurses had finally left me in peace.

"I could hardly leave you lying on the floor of my flat, now, could I?"

"I suppose not. But why are you still here?" I'd persisted.

"Do you want me to go?" Her voice had wobbled.

"No. I don't, but I want to know why you stayed, and why you came back."

"I don't know," she'd answered honestly. "I'm worried about you, and there's no one else, but ... it's more than that. Oh, I don't know. I just felt I had to, somehow."

"In that case, I'd like to ask you something."

"Of course, anything."

"I'd like you to come live with me." Going by the

look of incredulity on her face, you'd think I'd asked the impossible.

"I can't," she'd stammered. "I don't know anything about looking after a sick person."

"Good. You won't be looking after a sick person. I want you to help me put my stories in order, sort out what is still to be written and help me write them. Are you a writer or aren't you?"

We argued back and forth for days, when my strength allowed. It had been a battle, but my will was stronger.

The hospital had made it plain I was dying and my time was limited. Emma freaked when she heard the blunt statement of facts, but I assured her it was better to know the worst and prove them wrong, than to assume the best and get caught short.

"They will put me into some dreadful care place if I don't have someone at home. You heard them. Even you can't leave me to that fate, never mind what you think of me."

"But you have ... cancer!"

She could barely say the word; it scared her so much.

"Yes. And I'm going to die. I know that. So, I have to swallow my pride and admit I need help to put the last of my life in order. Will you help me?"

What I really wanted was to get her to face her demons before I succumbed. My demons had been faced years ago. I had fallen victim to them often, drifting in and out of clinics and hospitals, seeing psychiatrists and counsellors galore until I finally found solace in my writing. I understood mental illness and depression as well as any other victim and did not want Emma to become another statistic.

So days after my discharge, here we were learning to rub along together, trying not to stand on each other's toes, knowing there was an elephant in the room that couldn't be ignored for much longer.

"I'm not fussing. I just want you to rest. Now sit down and take this." She stood over me with a fixed glare, holding out a glass of water and my medication. Maybe I had met my match.

"I'd much prefer to carry on talking from where we left off," I mumbled through a mouthful of pills.

"We will. But later." She was adamant. "I haven't finished sorting the pile of notebooks in the back room. You take a nap and when you wake, I'll be ready."

They'd kept me in hospital for far too long, doing tests, sorting out medications and stabilising my out-of-control blood pressure, which had caused the collapse. By mutual avoidance, Emma and I had not raised the subject of the photo again, although it was uppermost in our minds. We both knew it would take time to work our way through the minefield that had brought us to this point. She was afraid of pushing me too hard. I had more patience and could wait for the right opportunity.

While I lay in the hospital, Emma had given notice at her flat and with little in the way of anything personal had moved into my spare bedroom at the same time they discharged me. Since then, she had started diligently collating all my notebooks into date order. I was always meticulous about entering the date at the beginning of a notebook and, when it was full, the end date, but I also began new notebooks before filling up older ones. Each of my authorial voices had their own journals. I never mixed them up, but even so, hers was not an easy task. Random thoughts could end up anywhere. I could usually remember them once I'd written them down. My memory was like that, but whether I could find them again in the notebooks was another thing.

In time, she would find the storylines, the character arcs, the date and place charts and the scenes all plotted out when she put it all together. She would find her story in one of my notebooks too. But, more importantly, she would find my history hidden amongst it, once I gave her the clues – which I would, before it was too late.

"Cup of tea, Charli?" she called, disturbing my reverie. "I'm dying of thirst after all that dust."

"Yes, please," I shouted back. "Then can we get back to it?"

We'd agreed she could use her nickname for me – she, because she didn't think she could break the habit: it had become second nature in everything she thought and wrote; and me, because I was used to it. Not that she and Luke were aware of their common pet name for me. They had met briefly, when Luke visited me in the hospital like any concerned old friend, but he and I were very careful. He had never come to the house on business in the past – that was how we'd kept our secret of my other identities for so long. We did everything through Michael, but I needed his help to sort out a future now Michael was gone. Even now, Luke rarely came to the house when she was there. If he did, they were uneasy with each other, as if each resented the time the other spent with me – except I sensed another undercurrent that I could work on.

Emma arrived with two cups of tea, placed one on the side table by my elbow and disappeared to return with a handful of books and a plate of biscuits.

"Now where were we?" I asked.

"I don't remember, but I've found something else that needs talking about first." She handed me one of my early journals. "Look at the date on the first page ... and the name."

I opened the fly page, almost prepared for what I would find, to see my youthful handwriting: *7 March 1960 – Georgie.*

I didn't say anything. What could I say? I already knew Georgie was the writer in me before Charlotte started. I'd simply chosen not to tell Emma.

"So, what do you have to say to that?" she demanded.

"She made me. Georgie always did have a lot to say, so I figured I'd better let her have her way."

"Stop trying to sound such a loony-tune. It won't wash with me. But are you telling me you wrote as Georgina Strong first?"

"Georgie insisted I had to get it all off my chest. She was my ally."

"Get what off your chest?" She sounded cautious, as if she thought she might be digging into uncharted territory.

I heaved a sigh – of relief or resignation, I

wondered. Now seemed as good a time as any. "I was diagnosed with bipolar disorder. I've had it since my teenage years."

"Oh shit. Sorry. I mean ... um. I don't know what to say. I've been ..."

"Insensitive?" I supplied as a possible ending to her sentence.

She flushed bright red.

"Now I'm sorry. That was insensitive of me. You weren't to know. I've deliberately kept it a secret for sixty years."

"Is that why you write so differently?"

"Of course. Amanda thinks the world is a place full of promise and hope, Georgie knows only heartache, misery and injustice in her world. Charlotte learnt to write in the world in between."

Wow. I don't think she actually said anything, but I'm sure that's what she mouthed.

"Back in a sec." Emma dashed out of the room to return a minute or so later with her notebook. She sat on the couch, pulled her knees up in front of her and, resting her workbook on them, wrote rapidly. Her natural self was emerging more and more as time passed. She no longer felt the need to dress immaculately all the time. When I first met her, she hid behind her appearance. The persona she put on when she dressed for work had formalised and distanced her from the task. Now in leggings and a long-line merino tunic, and with her hair getting longer every week, she looked youthful – energetic and keen.

"I need to write all this down so I can work out what the hell is going on," she gabbled as she wrote.

"No wonder I haven't been able to figure you out ... I've got a million questions."

"I don't think I've got time for a million," I said with as much humour as I could muster, "but I could probably manage a hundred for now."

"Charli! Stop it. I don't like you making jokes about dying. You know very well what I mean."

At least I'd raised a chuckle, I thought wryly. "Yes. I do. And we need to get down to it. Sit there quietly and keep writing. It's time I told you my story ... but I warn you, I want yours in exchange. I promised you that in your flat that day, before all this nonsense. I'll trade you. My story for yours. Agreed?"

She paled as she realised the magnitude of what we were getting into, with no idea where it might lead. I am sure she felt threatened, but if I'd read her right she would rise to the challenge.

She chewed her bottom lip and nodded. "Does this mean you will finally tell me about the photo?"

"I will, but not until the right time. That story has to come in sequence for it to make sense. But I promise you, once you know, there'll be things you'll need to do before you jump to conclusions and make judgments. I am relying on you to be the journalist you are and do your research – all of it. Do you understand me?"

Looking at Emma's stricken face, I started to feel like one of the mean characters from all those fairy tales: Red Riding Hood's wolf, Hansel and Gretel's witch, or the troll from the Three Billy Goats Gruff. But I stood my ground and she ... well, I can hardly say she accepted the terms, but she didn't argue either.

*****

We settled into a routine, becoming far more comfortable with each other than I'd expected. I ate little, but she was a great cook and could entice me to eat a few tasty morsels, which I wouldn't have done if left to my own devices. Every day we continued our talks, and I told my story. I left nothing out – except my birth name. Our time together was companionable, and I began to consider them the best times of my life.

Emma was a good listener. She cried sometimes when I spoke about the way my father had abused me, the murder of my mother and the gaping hole she left that I could never fill; and then my father's trial and subsequent execution. I tried not to give too many details, just to explain: the last hanging in England had taken place in 1964, seven years after my father, and the death penalty had been abolished in 1965. I tried to gloss over the minutiae to shorten the time frames. The rest she could look up if she wanted. I didn't want to relive them any more than I had to. She had the everyday stories of my life; now she was getting the stories I'd found so shameful when I was young.

The happier times when I was on the stage and the few years when my star shone brightly and I could pretend to be someone else offset the real misery of the rest of my early life. But when she realised I had been taken advantage of in my naivety, let down and abandoned by Tom – the one person I thought loved me – she completely broke down. I'd touched a nerve and wondered if something in her life mirrored my own, but we had an agreement: my story first.

I wove an amusing and diverting story of the journey by ship out to New Zealand and the culture shock awaiting me in a country twenty years behind the one I'd left. Then I also laid bare the loneliness of the boarding house and the home for pregnant women. I even managed to relive the birth of my daughter, but I couldn't tell her about the adoption process and the way my heart had been torn from me. I lied and simply said my baby had died. It seemed easier. I kept reminding myself I had a purpose in exposing myself to this extent, and I had to fulfil that purpose never mind what it cost me.

She became increasingly still as that part of the story unfolded.

"I can hardly believe it," she said in a hollow voice. "How dreadful. I never expected you to tell me anything like this. What an awful life."

She wasn't going to get away with that idea! "On the contrary," I said. "I've had a rich and fulfilling life. I owe my adoptive country a huge debt of gratitude. It gave me my life. It gave me choices I wouldn't have had if I'd stayed in the country of my birth. It valued me. I could be whoever I wanted to be, whenever I chose, because of that. The bald facts are just that, facts. Bad things happen to everyone at some time in their life, but there have been so many good things too. I have known the best kind of love – and I am rich beyond words. Living here in this house, with this view, and the never-ending cycle of life blooming outside my window, is perfect for me. I have the freedom to live in the real world or the worlds of my making, and thanks to my make-believe worlds, I am also a wealthy woman who has wanted for nothing – until now."

"How can you be so certain within yourself after all that happened to you?"

I realised she wasn't asking the question for my benefit, but for her own, and my answer was important.

"Because sometimes the best things come from the worst. You have to look in the darkest places to find the brightest light."

She didn't react in any way; her stillness unsettled me.

"Are you okay?" I asked. "Do you want to stop for today? Or change the subject."

She shook her head, rearranged herself on the couch, wiped her eyes and gave me a smile. "I'm okay. If you can do this, then so can I."

"See those roses bushes out there? All pruned back and waiting for spring. They are very special to me. Did you notice I use roses as my trademark?"

"Not to begin with, but yes, I did. Once I had all the books together. All different colours and styles."

"That's right. Amanda has a small red rosebud as her logo, I use a perfect deep pink bloom, and Georgina has a stylised full-blown yellow one with lots of thorns."

"But what have they got to do with it?" Emma asked.

"In my twenties, I was sick, mentally," I tapped my head. "It started with post-natal depression – not that they called it that in those days – and spiralled. I felt unworthy. In my life, people were always being taken away. I was left with nothing – and had nothing to give. I ended up in a black hole where no one should go."

She started to say something, but I stopped her.

"Let me finish. I started getting panic attacks. I'd shut myself away unable to go outside for fear something would spark one off, or the anger set in and I would rage at the world, screaming at anyone who came near me or tried to calm me. I was in and out of the mental ward at the general hospital and a frequent visitor to the mental hospital, but I got better. I found a way to thrive. The roses growing in the hospital gardens gave me hope. I would watch them burgeon through the phases of their life cycle. Each one different, but beautiful in its own way; each one with a purpose, even the rose hip that was left and the thorns that protected the blooms. I took each phase and wrote a story. Not about the rose, but about life."

I could see her flinch at what I'd just said. I think she recognised in herself what I had seen: the tears, the anger and, some days, the inability to do anything.

"Is that when Georgina started writing?" she asked.

I nodded. "Yes. I had to get rid of the anger about all the bad things that had happened to me and look at the good things life had to offer. It took a long time for me to see the good, but I did eventually, although it took many years."

"And that's when Amanda started to write," she hazarded a guess.

"It was. The rose is a perfect symmetry for life. The rose in full bloom exposes itself, ready to give up its life in the hope that good can come from it. It lays itself bare – just like I'm doing here – then the bees pollinate it and life starts again."

"And I'm supposed to be 'the bee', I presume."

"Only if you want something in your life to change. Which is why you came to see me in the first place, I suspect."

Emma

September

I had sat for weeks listening to Charlotte's life story – right through winter. I'd been alternately astounded, amazed, horrified and distraught in equal measures by the things she told me, but she also made me laugh. I could see why Charlotte the writer had become so popular: she could be funny when she wanted to be and added humour to the most bizarre events. Eventually, I realised that she could see right through me, and while she might not know the exact events that had brought me to where I was today, she knew there were parallels. She understood me better than I understood myself at times. Her experiences gave her insight to see the signs I didn't have a clue about.

Through it all, she was feisty and fearsome, and much braver than I think I would be under those circumstances. She wouldn't let me help her in any way. When the pain got too much – which it often did – she just disappeared to her bedroom. I didn't argue with her when she constantly refused radiation or chemo or whatever drugs they tried to push on her. When she wanted a glass of wine, or certain foods I knew would upset her, given her medication, I let her – it was her choice, not mine. As long as she ate and drank, there would be life.

I went with her when she wanted to go outside and walk in the garden – the beach was too far for her now. Or the odd time she got it into her head that she needed to go further afield. I'd take her in the car, and we'd go to the village shopping. She had no real need to do anything or go anywhere. I could have done it all for her, but this became her way of fighting the inevitable.

One day she suddenly announced, "I want to plant another rose."

"Why?" I asked, wondering how she thought she'd manage it. I suppose she expected me to do it, but I knew less about gardening than I could write on the back of a stamp with a paintbrush. "Haven't you got enough?"

"Probably. But this one will be special. I want a particular one in memory of Michael."

I tried to persuade her we should do it later, or I could order it online, but she was determined. We got in the car and headed to the garden centre where she demanded a deep red, scented rose bush called 'Loving Memory'. The assistant suggested it was rather late in the season, said he didn't have one in stock and tried to steer her to other plants. Charli let rip.

"I don't care about planting seasons nor do I want any other rose. I want this one and only this one. Do you understand me? I haven't time or energy to waste.

So just get me the one I want, young man, and do it now, or I'll report you to your manager."

I didn't have the heart to tell her he was the manager. He looked a bit put out but went away to check its availability anyway, while I persuaded her to sit down with me at the café to rest.

I ordered two cups of coffee and told her to relax while we waited. He came back within a short time, having sourced the plant and, much to my surprise, offered to have it delivered.

Charli became all charm and smiles as if another person had suddenly inhabited her body. "Thank you, young man. You have been most helpful, and I appreciate the trouble you have gone to."

This time a look of bemusement crossed his face, but he simply said, "Only too pleased to help, ma'am."

We'd slipped into an easy-going routine. I'd continued sorting her notebooks into order when she rested, but she had forbidden me to read them until we'd finished sharing our life stories. Then, she said, she would let me into their secrets. I didn't mind - well, maybe at first, but after a few quick peeks at some pages I decided I should wait after all. They didn't really make sense anyway and were far too disjointed, but I was entranced by some of the lyrical sentences she'd written.

We talked for hours, wandering off subject with anecdotes of her stage career, or memories of a summer's day, or a publishing mishap. I heard stories about her grandparents, where they lived and the sort of life they led, and whatever other snippet of history seemed to fit, going back even further into her past. She was a fountain of knowledge, which spilled forth in ever-increasing circles as we talked.

We spoke about the arts scene in New Zealand when she was my age and younger. She had a special interest in women authors such as Katherine Mansfield and Helen Shaw, and admired Ngaio Marsh's highly successful crime mysteries, even though she found them formulaic.

"I enjoyed – no, that's not quite the right word. Hardly enjoyed, but appreciated and understood, the writings of Janet Frame," she explained. "They helped put my problems into perspective. What I struggled with was mild in comparison. And later, in the eighties, I came to appreciate Reneé, the openly lesbian feminist author of the period who didn't start writing until the age of fifty. I figured there was hope for me yet, if she had found success late in life. Her play *Secrets*, which addressed sexual abuse within a family, resonated of course."

In the evenings, we'd watch TV if she was in the mood or listen to music, or we would read. She enjoyed me reading out loud to her from a book of her choice. For my own reading, I read more of Georgie's books.

Bit by bit, in her inimitable way, she diverted the subject from her and I found myself telling my story instead. One day, completely out of the blue, Charlotte asked, "Is there anything you remember about your grandparents?"

"No, not really. My grandmother died when Jinny was about fourteen or fifteen. Jinny told me she'd been ill for some time."

"Do you know what was wrong with your grandmother?"

I shook my head. I didn't have a clue.

"What about your grandfather? Do you remember him?"

"Not at all. I was only four when he died. Jinny said he was a distant father who left the running of the household to her, and she had free rein to pretty much do what she wanted."

"What did he do for a living?"

I shrugged. Again, I didn't have any idea.

"Do you remember any family occasions or did your mother talk about any extended family?" she queried.

"I don't think so. No, now I come to think of it. What I remember most is Jinny being on the move. I've told you about all that before."

There must have been a point to her questions, but she didn't let on as she fired more at me. How old was my grandmother when she died, and my grandfather – what was his age? How old was Jinny when I was born? By the time she'd finished, I realised how little I knew – and how much I'd deliberately ignored.

"And she never told you anything about your father?" Charli pressured.

"No. Nothing. I stopped asking in the end. Why all the questions?"

Charli boiled down what I'd told her into a few sentences. "So, if I've got the story right: she lost her mother at fourteen and was only seventeen when you were born. In which case, she would have been about twenty-one when her father died, totally on her own and with you to care for – what you were like at that age, and how you would have handled it?"

"Not well, I have to admit. But I blocked my mind to how difficult Jinny's life might have been. I was bitter and angry with her and didn't care. Selfish, I know, but aren't all teenagers?"

I'd also been on my own at twenty-one, but by choice. I thought I was indestructible and knew everything, but looking back I realised I had been extremely immature with no sense of responsibility. I'd lived a carefree life, when rules and timetables didn't suit me. How I got through uni was a miracle. I was disorganised and usually late with everything. But in the back of my mind, I knew I could run back to Jinny if, and when, my life fell to pieces.

"I never understood why she left her home when her father died. When I was older, I figured he might have left the house to her, or money at least. And even if the house was rented, she could have stayed there," I finished lamely.

"Have you any idea what upset her to set her off on her gypsy lifestyle?" Charli asked.

"None whatsoever," I snapped. "There's lots of things I don't know."

"Exactly, my point. I told you before we started that you would need to do some research if you were to make sense of anything. So there's your first challenge: find out about your grandparents. Now, tell me some more about Jinny. It's obvious to me she went in search of something. Love, maybe. Did you blame her for that?"

"In a roundabout way. I'd always been angry with her in some way or another. I blamed her that I never had any friends – not true friends – or anyone to rely on. I had plenty of kids to play with and loads of adults who taught me many things – things I didn't even realise I was learning until later, when I was much older – but I always felt insecure. I never knew which way she would jump next."

"Did she ever tell you stories of her past, or explain why she was doing what she was?"

Guilt filled my mind. I knew she had tried, and I had rebuffed her attempts. "I didn't listen," I admitted. "I really was an awful teenager."

"But what about earlier, when you were younger. Do you remember anything she said?" Charli persevered.

"I don't think so. Not much anyway. Nothing more than what I've told you. Why?"

"You need a starting point to work from. You can't go into your future without coming to terms with your past."

I lost my temper then. I didn't like being made to feel I was being unfair and unreasonable or, worse, that my feelings were unfounded. Jinny had left me and that was that. I needed no other reason.

"I know what went wrong. I don't need to go look it up. I hated moving, and she wanted to move again. We fought. I went off to Victoria University in Wellington and lived in a student flat – all by myself – the entire time I was doing my degree. I was determined to stay put and never move again until I was ready. I left Jinny to it. I wanted nothing more to do with her."

"When did you finish uni? And how many times have you moved since?"

"Dunno. Never thought about it. Um, I was twenty-one when I graduated." I started adding them up in my head. "Gosh. More than I care to admit: ten shifts in fourteen years."

"I thought so," stated Charli adamantly. "You have never really settled down, and you are still restless and fighting the world trying to find yourself. The only way you will do that is by sorting your past. Believe me. I've been there. I've lived in this house now for nearly fifty years and have been at peace. I've done it up and added to it when I've needed to, but it's more than a place to live, more than just a house. It's my home: the place I belong. It has stood me in good stead and holds many memories. Where do you belong, Emma? Think about it. Where do you belong?"

I felt my anger rising, but realised it was because I was embarrassed. Slowly, Charli wheedled out of me all the places I'd lived and why, and made me justify my decisions. The student flats were easy to talk about – others not so. I remembered when I'd met the bastard who would become my husband and ruin my life. I knew I would have to tell her about him soon, and all that had happened, but not yet. I was still hedging. I'd moved in with him and his other flatmates, then we moved to a place of our own. He changed jobs, and we moved again.

After we got married, I'd insisted we buy a place of our own and live there, forever and ever – happily ever after, in my mind. And we did, for five years, until Ruby was born. I couldn't live there after that and found my own place without him – without her – and ... I didn't know if I could follow Charli's example and talk about Ruby. Would I have the strength?

Instead I said, "I did a bit of flat sharing and moved on when someone I didn't like moved in."

Charli finished the list for me. "And since you've been in Auckland, there's been the flat I saw and now here with me. So much for staying put!"

She asked about my career and why I'd given it up to freelance or pick up fixed-term contracts. She challenged me to defend my reasons for shutting my mother out of my life and twisted the conversation around until we were back to who I'd been living with all those years ago, until I told her the truth. She didn't seem remotely surprised when I admitted Nigel had been a disaster, or that he'd been unfaithful and we were divorced.

"But that's not what is bugging you," she stated categorically. "Marriages end, but it's not the end of the world. If he had been the right one for you, you'd have got through all your problems together and come out stronger. No, there's something more. What is it?"

Charli's eyes bore into mine, defying me to sidestep the question.

Panic tore through me, and my heart thumped.

"I ... We ... My ..." I stammered, unsure how to get the words onto my tongue and out of my mouth. She waited, never taking her eyes off me. Pain bit deep in my gut. "My baby ... died."

Charli nodded, her eyes watered and her features softened. "I thought something like that might be behind it. Don't tell me more now. Tell me when you are calm, at a time when you feel you need to talk – and you will. But can I ask two things. When did your little girl die?"

"Three years, seven months and nine days ago." I knew the days and the hours almost to the minute. "And it still feels like yesterday."

"And your mother?" she prodded, her voice almost a whisper.

"A few months later."

I could no longer control my tears; they cascaded down my cheeks. My hanky was sopping wet in seconds, and Charli threw a box of tissues my way to help with the mop up. I couldn't talk about Ruby, but I could talk about Jinny. As I talked my anger grew.

"She'd wormed her way back into my life when I got married. She was the fun queen I remembered, and bit by bit I softened. I shouldn't have. As time passed, she became irrational and controlling, telling me what to do as if I were still a child. Then she'd take off again as she always had done. Going to find herself, she used to tell me – avoiding things, more like.

"She hated Nigel and wanted me to kick him out long before I had reason to, or knew I had reason to, at any rate. But she'd become a drunk. And she took drugs. I didn't want any of that as part of my life. The crowd she'd got into were all the same, and she was always off to parties somewhere. They had money too, and I'd hate to think where it all came from.

After Ruby ..." I gulped and stopped my thoughts in their tracks before I remembered too much.

Charli knew when to ask questions and when to let the story fall into place. Whether it was the author in her or her personal experiences, I couldn't tell, but I was grateful she let me talk at my own pace for as long as I wanted.

"Jinny was useless after Ruby died and kept muttering how it was all her fault. I didn't understand what she meant, but she got more drugged up and more drunk. I was an emotional mess and we fought, a lot. Sometimes she would stay at my flat – the one I'd moved to after I left Nigel. I couldn't bear being in the house where everything I'd ever wanted got trashed.

"She would suddenly disappear for days on end, but I couldn't cope with what had happened to me, let alone worry about my stupid mother. Nigel had cheated on me and passed on the disease that took my baby. I didn't care how bad he felt. I wanted him to suffer in hell, but even after all the bad blood with my mother, after all the arguments, I needed her to be there for me. I needed her to hold me as she had when I was little and smooth my hair, and promise me life would be good again. I wanted her to make it all better. But she didn't. She just didn't. Instead, she killed herself in a swimming pool, too drunk and drugged up to save herself."

I was almost screeching by this time and let the sobs take over. Whatever veneer I once had of the in-control, high-profile, tough-nut journalist was gone. I was a little girl again – and desperately in need of reassurance.

Charlotte

October

Spring is here in all its glory – and I'm still alive, although I am so weary. My rose bushes are thanking me for their early pruning and have fresh new leaves and dozens of buds, promising me a flowering before I pop out of this world. Even Michael's 'Loving Memory' has its first buds. Amanda usually comes to me with the spring, when the roses bloom and nature is full of promise, but I don't think I will have the facility to do her justice this year. She will have to wait a while.

Revealing our past is taking a toll on us both, but fortunately, Emma had no idea how much her story tortured me. I empathised with this woman I only knew as Jinny through a girl who was ostensibly a stranger but had got under my skin.

Emma was exceedingly upset after her angry outburst but now sat opposite me, looking drained and weary.

"I'm wondering," she began, "after all you've told me, whether Jinny suffered from mental illness. All those outbursts, the moving around, the moods, the drugs and alcohol – they all point to it, don't they?"

I was cautious in my reply. I knew these things can be hereditary and didn't want to frighten her. "I think they were her way of dealing with things she didn't know how to deal with."

She looked at me with dawning comprehension. "That's what this has been all about. You're worried I might have depression too, aren't you?"

"You could be prone to it possibly," I said satisfied.

Emma will work it out and survive, and when I give her the direction and let her into the secrets of my journals, she will have a future. I, on the other hand, need to try desperately not to die before my time.

I've sent her off to look into her grandparents' history, check some dates and bring me the storage file containing her mother's things. The one I strongly suspect holds the story of her life.

"Go on," I said, "I'll be all right on my own. You need freedom to do this research. It won't be easy and it will be time-consuming, so get on with it while I'm in a good mood."

In truth, I wanted her out of the house. I needed to talk to Luke, and he couldn't come while she was here. He knew he was losing me, and my going would add to the grief of burying his father such a short time earlier – but Luke was strong and he would be strong for me, I knew.

Luke and I sorted out my affairs in stages. He handled the lawyers for me, bringing me papers to give him power of attorney and other papers for my signature. I tried to remember to temper everything and take it slowly, so Emma wouldn't know what I'd been up to. Even so, the price I paid was high with all the effort it took.

Our most difficult conversation was over what I expected of him after I'd gone.

"Even you can't mastermind that!" he cried, but I'd offered him a bonus, a way of anchoring his position in the literary world if I was wrong. All he had to do was try. "Okay, Charli. Anything for you."

*****

Emma and I took up our regular places as the days lengthened and talked about her discoveries. I let her tell me all the details she had uncovered about her grandparents: their names, dates, where they were born, lived and died. She'd made one very puzzling discovery.

"My grandfather didn't die when I was four, which I'm sure is what Jinny told me. According to his death certificate, he died in 2001 in Nelson, where Jinny was living. I was in Wellington. Damn it! Jinny even lied to me about that."

"People usually have their reasons for lying," I said, fully aware of all the lies I'd told in my life.

"I know that. Don't be difficult, Charli. I need to find out why."

"Where were you born?" I asked, beginning to put together an unsettling picture.

She looked surprised at my change of tack. "Nelson."

"Didn't you tell me you often returned to Nelson?"

"Yes, most years. Maybe that's why. She went to visit her father. But then why wouldn't she take me? Why didn't I ever get to know my grandfather?"

"Do you have a copy of your birth certificate?"

"What? No. Why?"

"No reason. Just wondered," I flailed around looking for an excuse. "Most people have their birth certificate. You need it to get a passport."

"I've never needed a passport. I haven't gone anywhere. I told you, I like to stay put."

I didn't comment on her obvious piece of self-deception. The one thing she had not done was stay put. She may not have left the country, but all that moving around hadn't stopped her being as restless as bees in the honey pot. It was obvious to me if Jinny went back to Nelson regularly, while letting Emma believe both her grandparents were dead, the woman was hiding something.

"We may never know why Jinny decided to deliberately keep you away from your grandfather, but that was what she did," I told her. "There's no point worrying about it. Some mysteries are meant to remain and often are not as important as we first think."

I decided I should redirect the subject for a while and give her time to wonder about it. I felt sure she could find out more if she searched a little harder. "You've done a good job, Emma dear, very thorough. I knew you could. Now tell me, what have you found out about your mother?"

She handed me the still taped-up cardboard storage box.

"I haven't had the nerve to look."

Why ever not?" I heard my voice rising with surprise. "You must have been curious."

She shook her head and started biting her bottom lip, her trademark when she was nervous. "Not this one. There were other boxes with all her papers and bills, and stuff, nothing very important or interesting, which I waded through. I got rid of most of it."

"I'm amazed you've not been tempted sometime during the three years since your mother died."

Emma shrugged. "I was so mad at her for dying I didn't want to know anything more. She'd let me down, and nothing could rectify it."

"You've carried a lot on your shoulders in the last few years. It's time to shift some of it ... May I?" I asked diffidently – for me.

She nodded.

She sat in her usual place opposite me, watching. I could see the tension building again as she fidgeted, knowing she was nearing breaking point. Maybe I should tell her what I had done and leave her to work it out. Maybe then she could look at these things in the box. They were hers, after all.

I peeled the tape from the edges and lifted the lid. Gently rifling through, I could see some children's drawings, a few handmade birthday cards, a handful of photos and several important looking envelopes, which I assumed held insurance policies and maybe the all important life event certificates and the answers to all her questions – or were the questions mine?

"The photo," she dropped into the quiet sounds of rustling papers. "You have to tell me about the photo. It's eating me up. I can't stand it any longer. Please. I've been patient. I have. Please. Just tell me." Emma's voice wobbled.

I could no longer avoid her plea. The time had come to broach the banned topic of the photo. Now we'd got to the turning point, I didn't know if she was ready for what it meant. The photo could cause more pain and heartache, and she didn't need more of that. I looked up at the girl, who sat there holding her breath, waiting for the bombshell.

"All right. I'll tell you a story. Remember what I told you about the time I went to the home for pregnant mothers?"

"Yes. You hated it there, especially hated the matron."

"I did. But there's part of the story I haven't told you. My baby didn't die."

"What? Not you too. Why does everyone have to lie to me?" She glared at me, challenging, accusing. Nothing I said would change that fact: I said nothing.

"What happened to her, then?"

Immediately I was transported back to the very scene I had tried to block out of my mind for more than fifty-odd years. "She was put up for adoption."

*****

"I learnt they'd found a new home for my baby daughter and she would be leaving soon. I tried to give one of the nurses a little box as a gift for her adoptive parents, but she said Matron would never allow it. In desperation, I went to the midwife to ask for her help."

She said, "I'm sorry. Truly I am, but there's nothing I can do to help you, my dear."

"Please, just this one thing. Please?" I begged. "Please try."

I handed her the small box. On the underside of the lid was a small photo of a child in a white frilly dress wearing a bangle. Scrawled on the back in spidery, old-fashioned writing were the words: *For my Rose*. In the well of the box lay the same bangle.

"I have no influence around here, my dear. The matron won't have it, you know that. I don't know how to do what you ask."

I danced around her, stopping her from going on her way. I grabbed her arm, turned her around, jumped in front of her again, made her look me in the eye, trying to get her to see how important it was. I cajoled and wheedled until she laughed.

"Couldn't you ask someone else?" I begged. "Please? Someone in the office maybe, or the doctor, there must be someone higher up than the matron? Or can you give it straight to the new mother? Please? Let me give her a little memento. There's nothing to link her to me or anyone else for that matter. Think of it as a gift. It's no good to me any more, and it'll just remind me of her every time I see it."

"So who's that in the photo then?" she eyed me suspiciously.

"I have no idea." I lied, afraid that if she thought there was even a remote chance of tracing me through it, she'd refuse. I shrugged, determined not to crack and used all my acting skills. "I just saw the bangle in a shop one day and thought it was a pretty thing to give a new baby. I think the photo is there to show it's old and genuine gold."

She looked at it and then me, sighed, put the box in her pocket and went about her duties.

*****

"I never knew what happened to the box, the photo or the bangle," I said, to finish off the story. "But I had a second copy of the photo, a larger one. Ray and I had an argument over using some promotional photographs. I didn't want any. He insisted. He saw the old photo and stole it when I wasn't looking. He didn't even know who it was or its history, but that didn't stop him. The next thing I knew he'd produced those black-and-white promo shots with my signature on them. I could have killed him."

Tears were streaming down Emma's face. They had become the norm for many of our conversations these days: either her tears, or mine. We were a right pair of sobbers – if such a word existed – and it was beginning to annoy the hell out of me. I usually had much better control, but this disease had got the better of me, and she was so low, tears were her only outlet.

"Get a grip, girl. It happened decades ago. I've accepted it, so should you! Don't go getting upset over something when you don't know what it means." I was snappish now, knowing I wasn't being fair, but some memories are hard to dismiss.

She leapt to her feet and fled the room, leaving me gazing after her in exasperation. She was back within minutes, and it became my turn to be dumbfounded. She put a similar storage box to the one holding her mother's things on the floor and lifted the lid. Inside was like a shrine to her baby Ruby.

"I kept everything but hadn't looked at it once since I sealed it, until after Michael's funeral when I found the photo. This was Ruby's going home outfit," she gingerly lifted out a beautiful layette and laid it across my knee. "Her certificates are rolled inside these."

She took out two engraved silver cylinders. I presumed one was for the birth certificate and the other her death. There were numerous cards of welcome and condolence, some baby toys, a photo album and more clothes, all of which she spread out on the carpet around her. Then she took out a mounted frame with tiny baby hands and feet moulded in plaster and painted gold, with a professional photo of a newborn baby. It was enough to bring tears to my eyes.

"Here's where I found the photo."

With a trembling hand, she offered me the exact box I had described. The one I had given away.

I took it from her, almost afraid to open it, but when I did, I saw the photo inside the lid, knowing the inscription on the back said: *For my Rose.* The bangle lay nestled in its silk cocoon. Battered, worn and faded they may be, but I couldn't deny what I saw. I raised my eyes and looked at her – questioning, imploring, wondering what the hell was going on.

"Jinny planned to give it to Ruby, but she never lived long enough. I knew what it was as I'd seen it often enough when I was young, but Jinny'd gift-wrapped it with pretty pink baby paper and ribbons so I put it in this box unopened." She stopped and picked up the layette from my knee and hugged it to her before starting to load everything back in its box.

"I'd worn the bangle as a baby, Jinny told me, but I haven't looked at it for probably twenty years. When I saw the promo shot with your name scrawled across the bottom corner, I thought I'd seen the photo somewhere before. But it looked so different in black and white, and your name meant nothing, so I couldn't remember where I'd seen it, only that I had. It was only after we talked about Jinny that I remembered the box with the bangle and photo. It's the only photo I have that's that old. That's why I hid away, trying to work out what was going on."

Her intake of breath was audible; the tremor running through her body was visible; her pain was tangible.

"Who is she, Charli?"

*****

The photo was of my mother, and the bangle once belonged to her, her mother and her mother before her: an heirloom passed down from generation to generation. It had been mine. I tried to give it to my child and failed. I had lost my most precious possession as well as my most precious person. In those early days, after she'd been taken away, I soon learnt the only way to cope was to block everything out.

Now my heart was breaking all over again. How did Jinny have this box? I desperately wanted to believe my granddaughter stood in front of me, even while my head told me it couldn't possibly be true. This girl knew her history. She knew her mother's story and her grandparents, but there were gaps.

I'd always wanted to know what happened to my baby – my Rose. I wanted to know about her life, and if she had been happy, but I'd been too scared to go looking. If Emma's mother was that girl, then I had my answer: a long, loud, heart-wrenching no. All my guilt from those years flooded back. My heart wept at the thought I might have found my child's child, but by a cruel twist of fate would have her in my life for only a short time. My head, of course, told me to stop being a silly, emotional old fool. I pulled myself together to answer her question.

"I am not sure what all this means, but I can take a guess. There is only one way to be certain. Research. We need to look in your mother's box, and you need to find your birth certificate.

Emma

I got used to the long moments of silence following my questions as she drifted in and out of her memories, but they were becoming more frequent – and unnerving. The drugs were helping, keeping the worst of the symptoms at bay, but they left her dozy and she sometimes slurred her speech. She was fading before my eyes, but her tenacity and spirit kept her going. Her determination that I should know everything there was to know about her, about me, about her characters, and especially about Amanda, was unrelenting.

We'd spent hours together poring through the box belonging to my mother. We laughed over my childish drawings, and the simple but honest words of a child in a card had me drifting off into my past, remembering when I might have written them. We studied the photos and talked about who was in them, what they meant and where they were taken. She insisted I value them. They were my history.

Some of the paperwork was ancient and I could ditch it, some of it I hesitated over, unsure of its worth. Charli, as usual, gave me the best advice. "If in doubt, keep it. You can always throw it out later, but you can never get it back."

I put Ruby's box away, more at peace now I had shared her secrets. Charli was overwhelmed by the moulded hands and feet and kept running her hands across the glass as if she could feel them beneath it.

We both knew that with these delaying tactics we were preparing ourselves for the more official looking documents she'd seen at the bottom of the box. But eventually all that was left in the box were those grey-green, extra-long legal envelopes from earlier days. I reached for the top one.

Jinny had kept her mother's death certificate and tucked the much newer death certificate for her father inside the same envelope. Neither document revealed anything I didn't already know.

"At least she didn't lie about the year of her mother's death. She died of cancer. Ugly disease," I muttered.

Included on the certificate were the names of her mother's parents should I ever wish to follow the path into her ancestral roots. Her father's certificate confirmed what I already knew from the copy I'd got from the records office. It too had information about his parents and said he died of a heart attack. Neither certificate gave me any clues about Jinny.

Another envelope held her parents' marriage certificate – they had been married at St Michael's Church in Waimea West.

"I remember that church," I exclaimed, pleasantly surprised. "It's beautiful and so old. It's in the middle of nowhere really. I mean, it's in the country surrounded by farmland. We used to drive past it when Jinny had work out that way on one of the vineyards, or at the garden nursery."

I got my laptop out and searched for the image to show Charli. She read the details of how it became the successor to the first church in the Nelson province, built in 1866 to replace a smaller country church built in 1843.

"How wonderful. Details like these are gold to a story," she told me as she handed back my laptop. "At least this proves your family was Nelson based."

"Yes. No wonder Jinny kept going back. She must have grown up and gone to school there, don't you think? It was familiar to her."

Charli didn't answer. Instead, she handed me another envelope: old, but not as old as the other ones. I opened it.

"This is what we've been looking for – my birth certificate. No surprises here."

My date of birth, the year, the place and the mother were listed just as I had told Charli. The one remaining blank was my father's name, and any small hope I might find him through my birth record disappeared. There were simply no clues.

"This is the last envelope, Emma." Charli extended her hand with the documents towards me.

I took it from her and pulled out several papers. The first page I unfolded was the birth certificate for Jennifer Rose Wade. I didn't see anything unusual about it. Her name, birth date and her parents' names were all listed correctly. I handed it across to Charli and picked up the next certificate.

I must have made a sound because Charlie asked, "What is it, Emma?"

"It's someone else's birth certificate. This one's for a Rose, born in Auckland on the same day, and the mother is listed as Rose-Anne Thomas, whoever she is. I wonder why Jinny had this."

"Let me see," she croaked, waving her hand at me.

Something about her voice made me look up sharply as I handed that one over too. "Are you all right? You don't look good. I think you should rest now and we'll see to all this later."

Charli's hand shook as she took the certificate from me.

She stared at the second birth certificate as if her life depended on it, but said nothing.

I started to put everything back into the box.

"Wait. Don't do that just yet. Give me a minute." Her voice sounded weak and shaky.

"I really think we should stop," I said again. "Here, give me those and I'll put them away until you feel better."

Charli shook her head and gripped the papers tighter. I saw her screw her face up and wondered whether she was trying to stop herself from crying or whether the pain was getting the better of her.

"I'll get you some pills," urgency making my voice shrill.

"No. Wait. I want to say something." She paused to get her breath. "I want you to have my china cabinet."

The suddenness of her statement took me by surprise. I looked blankly from her to the cabinet and back again, dubious as to her motive and timing, but felt alarm settle in my stomach.

"Oh, no. I can't accept. It means too much to you. It should go to ..."

"Listen to me, Emma," she interrupted before I had thought of someone suitable she should leave it to. "I want you to have it. Now, before I go. Understand? You are right, it does mean a lot to me ... I've given this a lot of thought. It's not a harebrained idea that just popped into my head. I've made a decision, and I would very much appreciate it if you would honour my decision," she scolded.

Her face crumpled again.

"I promise to think about it, okay? But right now, you have to rest. We'll talk more when you're feeling better."

Charlotte

I am such a coward. Here I am, hiding in my room deciding what to say. I now know without a doubt that she is my granddaughter. That last birth certificate Emma handed me proved it. I am the Rose-Anne Thomas shown on the official record, but I honestly don't think Emma has any inkling.

I'm moved beyond words. My lifelong dream has come true. Even more so – to be able to see my great-grandchild's photo and her hands and feet have been incredible.

But how do I tell Emma? Should I tell her? Or is my desire to tell all the selfish instincts of an old woman about to die?

Behind the cabinet taped to the back is my original birth certificate and the original birth certificate for my daughter, Rose, along with her adoption papers. The girl, Jinny, must have gone down the official route to seek her birth parents – it was the only explanation for her having the document – and the box, but I wonder where the copy of the adoption records are? Maybe we missed them and they are still in one of those envelopes in the box. If they are and

Emma finds them, she will be extremely upset and, worse still, if she figures out I am the birth mother and didn't tell her, she will be angry with me. And rightly so!

I am so mad at myself for being such a confused weakling. In days gone by, this would never have happened to me. I would have hidden the past the way I always have done: denying everything and living by my made-up persona. But this cancer, this death sentence, has beaten me. I've reached the end of my life and have been taken totally unawares by the knowledge that I want something of me to live on. That's why I made sure Luke had the wherewithal to own the copyright for Georgie's books and gave him licence to the names. Georgie will die with me, but he's a clever boy and will make the most of my demise and make us famous again. It won't do his career any harm either.

I've already made my will out in favour of Emma. She will get my house, its meagre and aged contents, most of the money, as well as the copyright for Charlotte Day's books and Amanda's. Luke doesn't realise I've left him a chunk of money too, but he was the next best thing to a son to me and I need him to know I love him. How maudlin of me, but I could never tell him otherwise.

I just want Emma to accept the china cabinet while I can instil its history in her.

Emma

Charli refused to talk about the certificates or the papers we'd looked at the next time we talked but insisted I accept the china cabinet.

"Think of it as an early Christmas present."

"Okay, I give in. Thank you. Yes, I will accept, and I promise to love it as much as you have. I do anyway."

"Good. Now, since it is yours, I suggest one day soon you look at every item inside and if you don't know its story, then ask. That cabinet is full of history."

Once she'd settled that particular worry of hers, in her stubborn and unassailable way, she steered our conversations away from my troubles to her notebooks. She kept me so busy my mother's papers went completely out of my mind. There was nothing there to explain my past anyway, and what she offered was my future.

I soon discovered how she wrote her stories, how they linked together and how the character plots were developed. She showed me where the next stories were set and how they would evolve but left the endings for me to work out. I learnt to laugh again. Happier now

I could talk about Ruby whenever I wanted and know Charli understood, and I understood her better.

The weeks passed, October turned to November, and I noticed increasingly how she tired more easily. She spent a lot of time in her room, but she'd been insistent I start writing. Together, we started to write her memoir.

When she was resting, I wrote. Later, sitting in her chair in the front room overlooking her garden, with a blanket over her knees, she read, she critiqued and made endless suggestions and recommendations. I edited and rewrote the pages and we repeated the process.

We became a team. I came to rely on her, which was odd, since she relied on me to care for her, but my care only met her physical needs. Her care nurtured my spiritual ones. Charli, for all her faults – and she had many – had become my guide, my counsellor, my anchor, and I loved her. Much to my surprise, I loved that crabby, argumentative, sentimental old woman. I didn't think I was capable of love any more. Every ounce had been squeezed out of me. Not that I would ever say those words out loud to her. She would dismiss them as empty, saying deeds spoke volumes, better than any words, which were easy to say but not so easily lived up to. I felt sad she had lived a life so apart, without someone to truly love, but so much of what she had said to me earlier made sense now.

I still wish Jinny had told me who my father was, but it doesn't seem so important now I have Charli in my life. She has taught me that life goes on, and our journey teaches us to be more discerning, to be more caring and to adapt to whatever life throws our way.

Charlotte

December

I've decided. Emma has the right to know the truth about her parentage. She'll probably fly off the handle at me for not telling her as soon as I worked it out, but I can't change past decisions. What I can do is help her prepare for her future.

"Emma. Can you do me a favour please?"

"Of course. What is it?" She got up from the table by the window where she was writing and came to sit beside me.

"Did I tell you how pleased I am you've accepted the china cabinet as my gift to you for everything you've done for me?"

"Yes, more than once. Now stop going on about it."

"Well, it has more secrets than those I've told you so far."

With some protestation she followed my instructions and carefully unloaded the contents of the cabinet, setting them out on the table.

"It hasn't been moved in years, so I suspect it's

sunk a bit into the carpet. You'll need to be careful not to twist it so the leadlights don't break, but give it a good tug and it should move. Pull it out and look at what's behind."

A few minutes later, Emma had turned the cabinet sideways and began unpeeling the aged and brittle sticky tape holding a large envelope in place.

"What's this?"

"Open it and see."

She unfolded the wad of pages held together in the top left corner by a rusty paper clip. "What is all this ... stuff?" She waved the papers in the air. "Who was Rose-Anne Thomas?" her voice was now tinged with suspicion.

There was a long moment of hesitation.

"Me."

"What?" she paused, flummoxed – then clarity. "Are you saying ...?"

I nodded. "My Rose and your Jinny were the same person." My voice was so soft I'm not sure she heard me. She turned white, gasped and put her hand to her mouth as she read what was written. In my mind, I could see the bold, capital letters centred on the page with the words 'Adoption Certificate'.

"Jinny was adopted," she squeaked, as her eyes quickly scanned the legal details and clauses on the other pages.

Even she couldn't put into words what her mind was telling her, what I'd effectively just said. I was her grandmother.

We fell silent while we digested the implications, took in the ghastly reality of our situation and figured out how we would move forward from there.

"Go get your mother's papers."

She looked at me strangely but did as I asked. "Now, what's the date on the birth certificates – hers and the one for Rose?"

She scanned the pages and immediately understood my reasoning: Jinny received the information when Emma was four years old.

"The year we began our gypsy-life style," she answered. "The year she told me her father had died. That's why she went off. She was looking for her roots – looking for you!"

Emma turned and stared out the window, ran her free hand through her hair, clenched it tightly and bit her bottom lip. I waited while she read the pages again, but most of it was legalese with little further information.

"Why didn't you tell me sooner?" she demanded.

"I didn't know for certain until you showed me the second birth certificate. Then I had to make sure of my reasons. Was I telling you for my sake or yours, and should I tell you at all?"

"Of course you should have told me."

I could see her anger flaring. "I just did."

Much to my surprise, she pursed her lips and exhaled deeply as her anger deflated like a balloon. She sank onto the sofa beside me.

"You're my grandmother," she said, awe edging her voice. "I can't believe I have a grandmother."

"Well, I've not been much of a grandmother, whatever that is," I scoffed, trying for some levity. "More of a pain in the neck. But I'm grateful for the time we've had, even as friends. We have been friends, haven't we?" I wasn't confident of the answer.

"Yes," she answered spontaneously, getting up and giving me an awkward hug.

She looked at the papers again. "Did she know, do you think? Did Jinny know?"

"I think so. She had her original birth certificate."

"Hm, she wouldn't be able to get it from the authorities otherwise. Oh ... my ... goodness! I've just realised. She believed the photo of the little girl with the bangle was of her grandmother. And it was – but it was *your* mother not her adopted mother's. She was right. How amazing, but it's a pity she probably didn't know at the time."

"Somehow, my old midwife must have got it to Jinny's adopted parents and luckily, thankfully, the wonderful woman accepted it and gave it to Jinny as her birthright. I will forever be grateful to her. So should you. She must have been an admirable person. Find out more about your other grandmother, dear. For your own sake."

"I will, because Jinny did care for her. But there's still time for us to get to know one another better. There is. I'm sure there is."

I let her jabber. She knew as well as I that there was no time left. That is why I chose today to tell her.

"My time has come, Emma, dear. I can't fight this thing any more. Let me go."

"Don't talk like that, Charli. Don't, please. I'll look after you. You don't have to go into hospice." She clutched my hand tightly in hers. Mine was cold. Hers was warm.

"Yes. I do. You've been a wonder, but I will not be a burden on you. I've told you everything there is to tell. I've taught you as much as I can. It's up to you from now on. You can do it. I know you can."

"But I've only just found you. I can't lose you already. Don't go." Her voice rose at the end of every short sentence as she struggled not to cry.

"It's not the way I want it either. But we can't argue with fate. I'm happy to have known you, even if only for a short time, and I've lived to see my roses bloom once more, and for that I am grateful."

"Your roses! Who is going to care for your roses? You'll have to. Stay, please?"

I couldn't, I didn't have the strength. Neither did I have the strength to argue any longer.

"I have one last gift for you," I said, and told her where to find my hidden hoard of photos, sending her to fetch them and bring them back to me.

I unlocked the inlaid wooden box that had been my grandmother's, and on the top of the pile of photos was my copy of the one Emma had – the photo that in the end had brought us together. And together we went through them all, with me naming the people while she scribbled notes and put her lost history into order.

I had regained my most precious possessions: my child's child and my mother's bangle. This time I would give them away with a joyous heart.

Luke

I had watched Emma from a distance that day, respecting her privacy while sharing her grief. We were both grieving. I, not only for my father, whose spirit seemed everywhere, but also for Charli: my beloved Charli, the irascible, loyal, impossible Charli. The woman I loved most, second only to my mother. She had been around my entire life. She had joked with me, teased me, lectured me, sometimes even sent me to Coventry, as she called it, and wouldn't speak to me until I worked out on my own whatever problem I had. She taught me about life. She nurtured and loved me, cautiously, in her own way. I knew it. Dad knew it. We shared the secrets of her life, her books, her numerous names and her disappointments; there was little I didn't know. I think I was the only person – even better than Dad – who understood her, until Emma came along.

When the time came for Charli to go to the hospice, she left it to me and the lawyers to handle. We had her instructions: she hadn't wanted Emma to go with her or visit her, but Emma defied everyone. Every day, she and I sat by Charli's side, and I'm sure Charli knew she was there.

"Remember me fondly," she'd whispered with her last breath.

Charli recognised something rare in Emma. Even before she knew for certain who Emma was, Charli realised the girl needed help if she was to achieve her potential. She saw in her the same turmoil she herself had suffered. When Charli finally accepted the extent of her illness, she had shared all her concerns with me, making me promise to keep an eye out for Emma and help her in every way possible. She hadn't been tactless enough to directly tell me to 'set my cap' at Emma, as she would put it, but we both knew what she meant. If nothing else, I was to be her manager and agent.

I had watched Emma throughout the service and the mandatory post-service refreshments and only spoken to her at the last minute as the gathering was breaking up. Charli would have been surprised to see so many people turn up for her funeral, here in her garden with only a celebrant and friends, and where her ashes would be spread amongst her roses. She thought she was a recluse and unknown beyond a name on a book cover to most people. In reality, many people remembered her, admired her and came to pay their respects that day. Emma never for one moment expected to be considered chief mourner but was gracious and humbled by the honour naturally bestowed on her. I saw in those moments what Charli had seen in her.

"Perfect send-off. You handled everything very well," I said, extending my hand.

"Thanks, Luke. And thanks for all you did for Charli. She thought the world of you, you know."

Her hand was warm and soft in mine, and her smile reached her eyes: Charli's eyes.

"I thought she was pretty amazing too. Um ... this may not be the best time, but I have a message from Charli. Will you have a drink with me and I'll tell you what it is?"

I sensed a moment's hesitation. "By the way, Charli said I'm not allowed to take no for an answer."

Her laughter sounded like music, Charli's music.

*****

Now in the January, a little over two years after Charli's funeral, we are standing in her garden where her roses are blooming, with the same celebrant and surrounded by friends. This time we are celebrating the future and – at planting time – will plant a new rose in Charli's garden: a rose specially chosen because of its name, 'Heritage' – a strongly scented, soft pink bush rose notable for its perfect blooms. Charli would be pleased.

In the two years since Charli left us, Emma has met with great success. Charli planned it all, of course. She spent her last few months encouraging, cajoling and sometimes bullying Emma into doing what she asked. She showed Emma how to find and shape the stories in her notebooks and convinced her to write – as the one, but not only, Amanda Grove – and take advantage of her heritage. Charli gave Emma her own story.

As Charli had wanted, we released new editions of Charlotte Day's and Georgina Strong's novels, with fresh covers in print and as ebooks, at the same time as Amanda Grove released her new book. Emma was a nervous wreck, but I was not in the least concerned. As I expected, it became a best seller.

A year later, an unknown author by the name of Emma Rose released a novel – based on a memoir – that hit the Amazon best-seller rankings and rocketed up the sales chart to end up on the *New York Times* Best Seller List. Charli would have been delighted. I had a sneaky feeling she had masterminded the whole thing after all.

I look around the garden, taking in its charm. Emma stands beside me, looking beautiful in a peach dress to match the rose she'd chosen for her author logo, holding our child in her arms. I am aware of the celebrant's voice reciting the words we had written and take a small box from my pocket in readiness.

As the words I am expecting are spoken, I feel Charli's presence. Surrounded as we are by the perfume from her precious roses, I slip the tiny gold bangle that once belonged to her – and generations before her – onto the wrist of her great-grandchild: Rose Charlotte Grainger.

I could hear Charli's voice. "*Live well, my sweet Rose.*"

When the last rose of summer fades away, so a new life begins, and the cycle continues.

Children Learn What They Live

If children live with criticism,
  They learn to condemn.
If children live with hostility,
  They learn to fight.
If children live with ridicule,
  They learn to be shy.
If children live with shame,
  They learn to feel guilty.
If children live with encouragement,
  They learn confidence.
If children live with tolerance,
  They learn to be patient.
If children live with praise,
  They learn to appreciate.
If children live with acceptance,
  They learn to love.
If children live with approval,
  They learn to like themselves.
If children live with honesty,
  They learn truthfulness.
If children live with security,
  They learn to have faith in themselves and others.
If children live with friendliness,
  They learn the world is a nice place in which to live.

This is the author-approved short version.

THANK YOU

I hope you enjoyed reading this story.

It would be most helpful if you could please visit
www.amazon.com/Vicky-Adin
and write a CUSTOMER REVIEW of the book.

Constructive comments are always welcome, and
if you would like to receive information on my new books
please email me on vicky@vickyadin.co.nz
with BOOK ALERT in the subject line.

* * * * *

Sign up for my newsletter to keep in touch
with things I'm doing
www.vickyadin.co.nz
and find my books on Amazon at
www.amazon.com/Vicky-Adin

See my other books
on the following pages

* * * * *

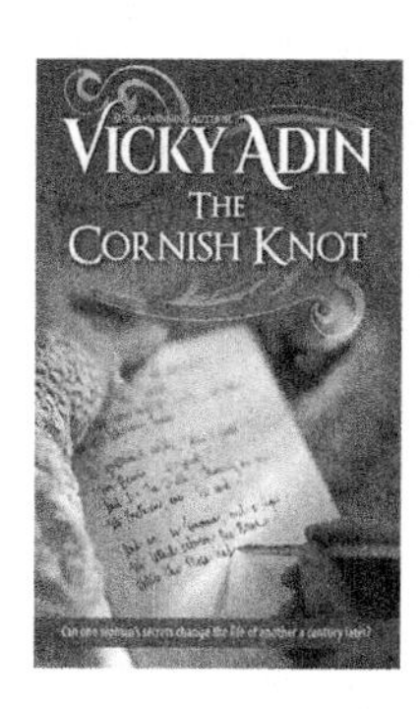

The Cornish Knot

Can one woman's secrets change the life of another a century later?

(Set in Cornwall, Italy and New Zealand)

On the anniversary of her husband's unexpected death, Megan sits at home heartbroken and disconsolate. A mysterious package arrives containing a journal written a century earlier, which shakes her out of her self-imposed seclusion.

She embarks on a journey following in the footsteps of the journal's author, from New Zealand to Cornwall, France and Italy, uncovering a past she knows nothing about. She is pursued by a much younger man in Venice. She meets an intriguing fellow countryman in Florence and finds herself caught up in the mysterious world of art and captivated by a series of unknown paintings. As she unravels her history and reveals its secrets, can she also find love again?

An engaging tale of grief, loss, love and family intrigue ... wonderful story, and a real page-turner, which leads the reader through all the twists and turns of a well-constructed plot. I loved the insightful descriptions of family relationships, the fully realised characters and the various locations in which the action takes place. Seldom have I read such a poignant and faithful account of the effects of bereavement. I can't wait to read more. **** 4-star Amazon review

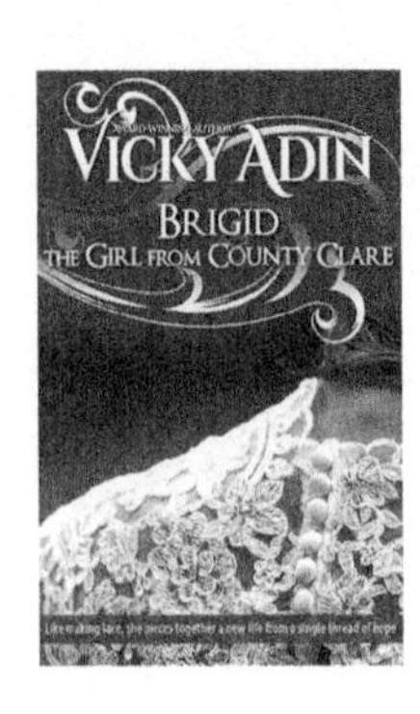

Brigid
The Girl from County Clare

Like making lace –
she pieced together a
new life from a single thread of hope

(Set in Australia and New Zealand)

Brigid is torn. If she stays in her beloved Ireland, she is another mouth to feed in a land plagued by starvation and poverty. If she leaves, she will never see her family again. But leave she must. There is not enough food.

Heartbroken, she boards the ship that will take her to a new life in Australia, comforted only by the knowledge that her cousin Jamie will make the journey with her. Her skill as a lacemaker soon draws attention, but life doesn't always run smoothly in the harsh new landscape. Brigid must learn to conquer her fears and overcome the stigma of being a servant, a female and Irish if she is to fulfil her dream.

A new start in New Zealand offers hope – until the day she encounters the man who seeks her downfall.

The historical aspects of the story are so accurate and described so perfectly that the reader will frequently need to remind herself/himself that the story is fiction ... This is a thoroughly satisfying read. It is the kind of story that passes the test as a work of history, and is equally satisfying as a novel that will have your attention from first to last. **** 4 stars – Frank O'Shea, *The Irish Echo*, Sydney

----

Winner Indie B.R.A.G medallion and
Chill with a Book Readers' Award

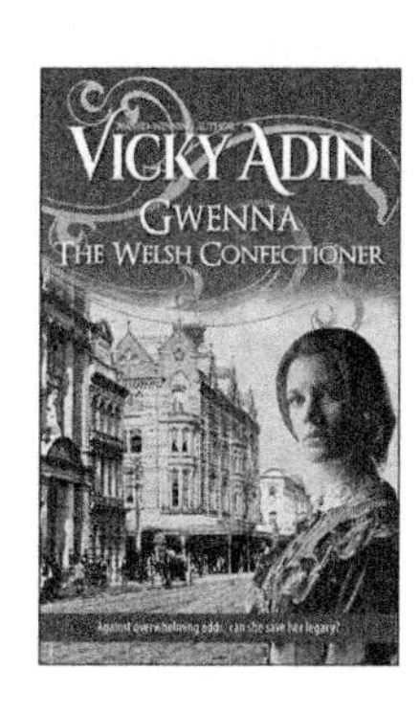

Gwenna
The Welsh Confectioner

**Against overwhelming odds,
can she save her legacy?**

(Set in New Zealand)

Amid the bustling vibrancy of Auckland's Karangahape Road, Gwenna Price is troubled. For all her youth, she has become the master confectioner in the family business since her father died. She promised to fulfil her Pa's dreams and open a shop, but with her domineering and incompetent stepbrother Elias in charge, the operation is on the brink of collapse.

In an era when women were expected to stay at home, Gwenna is a plucky young woman with uncommon ambition. She is determined to save her legacy. Despite the obstacles put in her way, and throughout the twists and turns of love and tragedy, Gwenna is irrepressible. She refuses to relinquish her dreams and lets nothing stand in her way.

Utter brilliance. I was captivated from beginning to end. Vicky really brings the characters to life and you can really engage with what it must have been like to be a young girl like Gwenna going into business at the turn of the century in a male dominated society. I was totally engaged with every character, each one contributing to make this a truly wonderful story; my only disappointment was when it ended. This is the first book I have read by this author but it won't be my last. ***** 5-star Amazon review

Winner Indie B.R.A.G medallion, Chill with a Book Readers' Award and Gold Standard Quality Mark

The Disenchanted Soldier

From soldier to pacifist

Based on a true story

In 1863, young Daniel Adin, a trained soldier, embarks on an adventure of a lifetime. In pursuit of a new life and land to farm, he travels to New Zealand to fight an unknown enemy – the fearless Maori.

A hundred and thirty years later, Libby is fascinated by the stories of Daniel, who looks down at her from the aged black-and-white photos on the walls. She wants to know more, to know what he was really like, but Daniel's story was more than she had bargained for.

A great insight into the lives of a family and what was going on around ordinary people in the early days of colonization.

– Ged Martin

I loved this book and so will you if you like historical fiction and family sagas set somewhere you likely know little about. This is beautifully and sensitively written. The characters are terrific. The fascinating part to me was how Vicky was able to take us on the family's journey in a thoughtful and non-judgmental way.

***** 5-star Amazon review

Printed in Great Britain
by Amazon